THE PAY-OFF

Vivien Armstrong titles available from Severn House Large Print

Beyond the Pale
Bird of Prey
Fly in Amber
Fool's Gold
Murder Between Friends
No Birds Singing
Rewind
Smile Now Die Later

THE PAY-OFF

Vivien Armstrong

Severn House Large Print
London & New York

This first large print edition published in Great Britain 2006 by
SEVERN HOUSE LARGE PRINT BOOKS LTD of
9-15 High Street, Sutton, Surrey, SM1 1DF.
First world regular print edition published 2005 by
Severn House Publishers, London and New York.
This first large print edition published in the USA 2006 by
SEVERN HOUSE PUBLISHERS INC., of
595 Madison Avenue, New York, NY 10022.

British Library Cataloguing in Publication Data

Armstrong, Vivien
  The pay-off. - Large print ed.
  1. Police - England - Oxfordshire – Fiction
  2. Russia (Federation) - Antiquities – Fiction
  3. Detective and mystery stories
  4. Large type books
  I. Title
  823.9'14[F]

  ISBN-13: 9780727875358
  ISBN-10: 0727875353

Printed and bound in Great Britain by
MPG Books Ltd, Bodmin, Cornwall.

One

A chilly Sunday afternoon in late December is a bitter companion for any sort of walk but especially for an unlooked-for trudge through country lanes with no habitation in sight.

Tessa Cox's car had broken down two miles outside Bartram and a lowering sky hung like a pall, threatening rain. She called Lulu on her mobile but the number was engaged, probably off the hook, which didn't surprise her, her elderly friend Lulu Starewska being fiercely defensive of her Sunday afternoon naps. But there was no help for it. Tessa's anxiety ballooned like the storm clouds massing on the horizon; tomorrow would be too late. She locked the car and set off at a brisk trot.

Lulu Starewska's cottage stood squarely on Bartram village green behind the bus stop, its front door opening straight on to the street. Old bricks under the thatched roof were streaked with mossy stains, the curtains at the front windows already drawn. Lulu's ancient MG was neatly parked under a ramshackle lean-to at the side of the house but Lulu had clearly shut up shop to visitors and put the phone on hold.

The village was still technically within the estate of Bartram Court, a National Trust manor house now closed for the winter, but the tied cottages had been sold off to incomers, the locals preferring the convenience of the new council estate close to the main road to Oxford.

How Lulu, an irritable old woman, had become an accepted fixture in Bartram was a mystery. Tessa wondered if she wore her eccentricity like invisible chain mail to fend off familiarity. It had not worked. Curious neighbours sought out the chinks and, despite Lulu's atrociously rude manner with strangers, she had, over the years, evolved into a sort of gargoyle they were fond of, proud of, in fact, convinced that the flamboyant old trout's hidden London life was a starry round of the celebrity circuit, Lulu's acerbic press comments and occasional television rants in which she rubbished the latest New Art Sensation only strengthening her Bartram friends' determination to preserve her privacy at her weekend retreat.

Tessa reached the Green as the first

hailstones fell. She ran past the village duck pond and banged on the door, her hair streaming, the hailstones ricocheting off the windows like grapeshot. She didn't waste time knocking, the door was unlatched, as always, Lulu's outlandish response being that 'At my age, darling, a rapist would be a bloody godsend.'

Tessa called out. 'Hello? Lulu? It's me, Tessa. I must speak with you – it's urgent!' She hurried through to the sitting room, mouthing apologies, anticipating the cross-fire.

But the room was empty, the place eerily silent. Surely she wouldn't be out in this awful weather?

She pushed open the kitchen door but under the harsh glare of the unsparing strip lighting, the scene of horror was all too clear. Lulu lay in a pool of blood; her cat, Pushkin, crouched in the shadows, mewing piteously.

Two

The police arrived at speed, two squad cars and a posse of uniformed men shattering the afternoon torpor of Bartram. The summer months would have been different, the place humming with families relaxing on the village green after a tour of the big house, kids crowding round the ice-cream van that parked by the bus stop every Sunday afternoon.

The senior officer hurried across to the uniformed sergeant scrambling from one of the squad cars. Detective Chief Inspector Hayes, a tall man who, it was rumoured, enjoyed a certain vulpine appeal to the ladies not shared by his team, who regarded Roger Hayes as a boss with a short fuse and abrupt manner. His transfer from Oxford only two years previously had not been greeted with universal acclaim in the canteen but Superintendent Waller had to admit that the bloke had a deft way with suspects and had already notched up a couple of high-profile successes on the crime rate records.

Hayes confronted the sergeant guarding the front door. 'Right, Preston, before we go in, who've we got on the call-out?'

'DS Bellamy's on his way, sir, and there's two detective constables and that new girl, DC Robbins.'

'The redhead?'

'That's the one, sir, very quick off the mark – she was involved in that last case in Bramley Green, if you remember. And the SOCO team should be here any minute.'

'And the lady who made the 999 call?'

'A Mrs Cox, sir. She's with the neighbour,' he said, indicating the green shutters of Ferry Cottage.

The brief hailstorm had given way to rain, the afternoon already closing in, defeated by the dismal combination of winter weather. Hayes pushed a hand through his wet hair, pausing to calculate the effectiveness of the scratch team at his disposal. An old woman killed in her own home: it was the sort of scare story to bolster the already strident demands for more effective policing in rural backwaters like Bartram, and Hayes had no taste for defensive parries with an inevitable media outcry. What he was yet to discover was that the victim, far from being an unimportant old biddy, was, in fact, a lady with a certain celebrity, in the arts field at least. He sighed and, after a swift assessment of the location of the cottage in relation to the village green, crossed the threshold of Star Cottage.

The door was still unlatched, the hallway dark, but several lamps lit up the empty sitting room and fiercely bright overhead lighting illuminated the kitchen. The door stood open, the body almost hidden by a tablecloth sagging on to the floor, broken crockery and the remains of a meal littering the stained terracotta tiles.

Hayes paused in the entry, assessing the scene with a coolness Sergeant Preston himself found difficult to comprehend. The place was a bloodbath. The kitchen was small and cramped with furniture. A deep ceramic sink under a window overlooked the back garden and oak cupboards ranged above a scarred wooden counter; a pine dresser set with mismatched pottery plates and mugs occupied too much space along one wall.

The old woman lay spread-eagled, one ringed hand clutching at an auburn wig, which had tumbled to one side hiding her face, grey wisps of her own hair veiling the scraggy neck. Scrawny legs protruded obscenely like drumsticks from beneath her skirt, and Hayes guessed that the sad victim of this vicious attack must have been at least eighty years old.

Blood had pooled around the body and spattered the shards of broken china strewn around. Sanguineous runnels seeped between the floor tiles and blood splashed in a great arc across the back wall.

'Blimey, who'd have thought she'd have all that blood?' Preston said with a gasp, his face yellow under the unforgiving strip lighting.

A single footprint in the dried blood caused Hayes to pull back. 'We'll wait for SOCO to photograph this. You stay at the front door, sergeant, I'll take Jenny Robbins next door to question the witness. Mrs Cox, you said? Tell Bellamy to call me when the forensics team gets here and for Christ's sake get this cottage cordoned off before any nosy neighbours start peering through the curtains. That track at the side – is it a public footpath?'

Mike Preston nodded. 'A bridle path mostly used by riders, too churned up for ramblers – leads down to the river.'

'You know it?'

'My youngest used to crash around down there on his mountain bike with his mates but I put a stop to it after complaints from the dog walkers back in the summer.'

'Right. Well, let's have a dekko before the doctor gets here. No question of the lady not being dead but I presume he has been called out?'

Hayes carefully stepped round the body and bent down to see what he could of her face, half obscured as it was by the tumbled wig. 'Good God! Look here. The poor cow's had acid or something thrown in her face. We've got a bloody maniac on the loose.'

The cat started to yowl and the sergeant glanced away, the sight of the old woman's blistered cheek turning his stomach.

Hayes rallied. 'Get that animal out of here!'

Preston knelt down to grab the cat but it drew back, hissing, its yellow eyes narrowed to venomous slits.

'It can't seem to move, sir. Its fur's all matted. I think it must have caught some of that acid an' all.'

Hayes stiffened. 'That's all we need. An old lady and her moggy attacked in her own kitchen on a quiet Sunday afternoon. All the ingredients of a real sob story. Leave it. I'll go next door and see if the neighbour'll take it in. You put the skids under the doctor, tell him to get over here at the double.'

He retreated to the hallway and made a beeline for Ferry Cottage and the unfortunate Mrs Cox, whoever she was. He offered up the slim hope that his witness would not be reduced to hysterics by what, by anyone's standards, was a traumatic discovery: the body of a friend who had not only been knifed in a brutal frenzy but possibly tortured first.

Three

The neighbour at Ferry Cottage quickly came to the door, regarding the tall detective and his red-headed sidekick with relief.

'Thank God you're here. Whatever's happened? Tessa's still in shock – hardly spoken a word, just said Lulu's been viciously attacked. Is she dead?'

'I'm afraid so.'

The woman brushed away their ID cards and led Hayes and Robbins inside, her eyes wide with alarm. She wore khaki combat trousers that loosely hung about her ample thighs like camouflage, a maroon sweater – presumably her husband's, Hayes surmised – cladding the top storey. He assumed her to be in her mid-fifties, though he felt himself to be out of his depth with women's ages, especially those women who eschewed the make-overs Pippa, his current girlfriend, assured him made any snap assessment as random as the bonus number popping up at the end of a winning lottery sequence.

She closed the door behind them and marched through to the sitting room. Ferry Cottage was a bigger version of her neighbour's house and must have been extended, the living area spacious despite an inglenook fireplace that occupied most of one wall. A log fire burned in the grate, the heat in the room enfolding the new arrivals like a blanket.

A young woman perched in an armchair by the fire, her head wrapped in a towel and her arms clasped to her chest in a defensive embrace. She shivered despite the temperature and, after a glance at Hayes and the girl, resumed an intense focus on a burning log that suddenly rolled into the hearth in an explosion of sparks.

The older woman leapt forward and kicked the log away to one side. 'This last lot's been nothing but trouble. Green. Unseasoned wood always spits.' She turned back to the inspector, touching her mouth in a gesture of despair. 'My name's Dolly Froude, by the way.'

Hayes nodded and approached the shivering ghost seated by the fire. 'Mrs Cox?'

She raised her head.

'I'll fetch us some tea, shall I?' Dolly suggested and hurried out of the room, leaving Hayes and Jenny Robbins to break the ice

15

with their traumatized witness.

He pulled up a chair and sat close. 'Mrs Cox, I know this is difficult but we need some essential facts before we can begin to find out what happened. Do you feel up to answering a few questions?'

Tessa let her hands fall into her lap and regarded Hayes with a level gaze. She was, he decided, still in shock but strangely tearless. Clearly, a strong personality. His luck was in. A sensible statement from this one would be a head start. Jenny Robbins remained in the shadows, as still as a sentinel, knowing that an intrusion into the boss's handling of a tense situation would only earn her an earful of abuse once they got back to the station. She had worked with Hayes before and had learnt to tread softly. She took out her notebook.

'Shall we begin with the details? Your full name and address?'

Her voice was low, the cultivated tones of an educated woman, only the tremor in her delivery exposing a persistent state of horror. 'Tessa Cox. I live at Woolpack Farm, Trimmingham, five miles away from here – you probably know it. It was my parents' house. I was brought up there. Tony and I moved back after we married.'

'Which was?'

'Four years ago.'

'Have you telephoned your husband? He's on his way?'

'No. Tony's abroad. On business.'

'There's no one at home with you?'

'Not at present. I hoped to see Lulu before she went back to London tonight.'

'Ah. The lady next door.'

She nodded. 'Lulu Starewska.'

'She was expecting you?'

'No. It was a sudden decision. I rang but Lulu had taken her phone off the hook. She often did that at weekends. She called the cottage her oasis. I can't believe anyone would harm her, it's not as if there's anything to steal.'

Hayes persisted. 'You were not related? The lady was just a friend?'

'A business acquaintance. I sometimes worked from home for Mrs Starewska.'

'In what capacity, Mrs Cox?'

'I'm a conservator. Lulu often commissioned me to clean or repair paintings for her. She has – had – a gallery in Kensington, the Star Gallery, you may have heard of it. Lulu specialized in amber and Russian icons, but the gallery sold lots of decorative things, oriental screens, tapestries, that sort of thing.'

'And you arrived at what time?'

'It must have been about four o'clock but I'm not sure ... I phoned the police straight away, I knew there was nothing I could do...'

'You went into the kitchen?'

'Not really. Just a step or two to lift the tablecloth – so I could see if it was just a bad fall. But all that blood—'

She started to tremble and Hayes looked quickly over at Robbins, who shook her head.

Dolly Froude returned with mugs of tea and Hayes relaxed, glad of a little respite, deciding that his anxieties about the investigation were unfounded. An elderly lady gets mugged by an optimistic thief who turns ape when he finds out the place, contrary to rumours in the village, has no valuables or stack of fifties under the mattress. But a local would know she was only a weekender, wouldn't he? Why not break in midweek when the place was empty? He shrugged. An opportunist then who watched the old woman from the bus shelter, thought he was on to a winner? A quiet Sunday, no one about in this bloody awful weather ... Pretty run of the mill stuff. Except for the acid. Acid was nasty. Acid was not normal stuff for a sneak thief to have in his back pocket, was it?

He accepted a mug from Dolly, watching

the colour come back into Tessa Cox's cheeks as she sipped her tea.

'Mrs Starewska kept none of this valuable artwork at the cottage?'

'No, never. She sometimes brought down a painting for me to see and left it at my studio at the farm but she preferred to keep her London life entirely separate.'

'Lulu was often on the telly,' Dolly interjected. 'She made no bones about rubbishing that arty crowd running the 'New Wave' as she called it. A real tartar once she got on one of those discussion programmes. I think they booked her just to give the show a bit of a bang.'

'She had enemies?'

'Well, not exactly enemies, inspector, just a few art critics who found her outbursts insupportable,' Tessa insisted. 'Lulu has rather old-fashioned ideas about art and the TV people liked to wind her up. She had no dimmer switch, inspector. Lulu Starewska was always full on.'

Hayes nodded, deciding this his initial mental picture of this elderly victim had been right off the mark. Before he could pursue the loose ends there was a knock at the front door. Dolly hurried out and brought a constable into the room.

'The SOCO team's arrived, sir. When

you're ready they'd like a word.'

Hayes jumped up. 'OK. I'll be right there.' He excused himself and spoke quietly to Robbins before turning back to Tessa Cox.

'I think we must postpone this conversation for the present, Mrs Cox. May I phone you later and speak with you at home? You have your own transport? Or would you like my constable to drive you home?'

Tessa suddenly looked confused and pulled off the towel wrapping her hair, shaking out a surprising volume of damp brown curls. 'Christ, my car! I'd forgotten. It broke down just by Whipps Wood.'

'You walked here? All the way? In the rain?' Hayes spluttered.

'Well, yes. I needed to see Lulu. Whipps Wood hardly boasts a taxi rank, inspector,' she added with asperity.

'We'll discuss this later,' he retorted, anxious to get back to the murder scene. 'In the meantime, DC Robbins will drive you home, unless you prefer to stay on with Mrs Froude.'

'*Miss* Froude!' Dolly irritably put in before turning to the girl. 'Stay, Tessa, you've had a terrible shock. You don't want to be alone in that big empty house.'

'Thank you, Dolly, but no. It's very sweet of you but if I could get back I'd rather go home. You've been more than kind.' She resolutely got to her feet and struggled into a wet mackintosh hanging on the back of the chair.

Hayes nodded at Jenny and made for the door. As he was about to disappear he turned back to face the women.

'Actually, there is one problem. The cat. Mrs Starewska's cat's been injured. Needs a vet. Would one of you kind ladies take it on?'

Four

Hayes was hailed en route by the police doctor, Charlie McKenna, who waited, leaning against the bus stop, smoking a cigarette.

'Hayes! Hello there. Nasty case you've got with this one.'

They shook hands and moved into the deserted bus shelter.

'Nice to see you again, Charlie. How was the sabbatical, you lucky dog?'

'Why should these teenagers be the only ones to grab a gap year? Been back a week now, but I'm still trying to rev up.'

'You took your wife on walkabout, I hear.'

'Yes. We pottered about in France for the winter then bought a boat and bummed around the Greek islands. You should try it.'

Hayes laughed. 'Chance would be a fine thing. And if you'd stayed away much longer, mate, we'd have been too cosy with Doctor Flanagan to let you have your old job back. Sorry to have broken up your first weekend at home, Charlie, but you were able to take a look before SOCO arrived?'

'Just a peep. The pathologist will need to examine the poor lady in detail.'

'But you have an opinion about the time of death?'

'Give or take a couple of hours either way, I'd say ten or eleven last night.'

Hayes' jaw dropped. 'Last night? I thought she'd been attacked today – Sundays are quiet round here off season once the big house is closed for the winter. Are you sure?'

'A thatched cottage retains the heat and she had off-peak electric rads boosting the temperature but, yes, on balance, I'd say the killer struck on Saturday night.' He stubbed out his cigarette and attempted to set off back to his car, which was parked on the edge of the Green.

'Hang about, Charlie. The acid? You think the burns were inflicted before death?'

'Difficult to say. But probably, yes. A corrosive of some sort, possibly battery fluid, but an analysis would settle the matter. Grisly. The knife wounds were decisive and, in my view, struck in fury, no hesitation there, no teasing cuts. Mercifully quick at the end. An old woman like that didn't stand a chance and the thick walls would deaden any screams or cries for help. No pub on the Green, I see, just a sub post office, no chance of a passing crowd turning out at closing time noticing any prowlers.' The doctor buttoned his coat. 'Let me know what the pathologist turns up, will you? He'll be more in a position to give you a full report.'

Hayes let him go, thoughtfully regarding the car's bumpy progress across the grass, setting off the ducks on the pond in a raucous farewell.

Saturday night? After dark. But would an old woman admit a stranger so late? There appeared no forced entry but a cursory glance round was no good, was it? Hayes decided a meticulous examination of the cottage would be imperative.

He hurried into the hall, keeping his hands in his pockets, eyeing with impatience the forensic crew in their protective clothing. Sergeant Stan Taylor beckoned him through to the kitchen door and they glumly reviewed the harrowing scene.

'What's the verdict, sergeant?'

'No weapon. No empty bottle of acid and, so far, not much in the way of fingerprints. You've interviewed the person who found the body?'

'A Mrs Cox. Some sort of business associate of the deceased. Called in on spec, so she says. I'll get fingerprints for you for elimination but she says she came through to the kitchen, pulled aside the tablecloth, but touched nothing else.'

The sergeant pointed to the pattern of blood spattered across the back wall. 'The killer must have hit an artery. The doc counted six deep cuts to the body, an effective blade, possibly a hunting knife, but no sign of defensive wounds, not that an old lady could put up any sort of a fight. Do you know her name?'

'Starewska. Lulu Starewska. A gallery owner who spent only weekends here. No family on the scene so far but Mrs Cox seemed to know her pretty well so we can fill in the details later. How much longer will you be working here?'

'Not much more than another hour or so. We've taken a stack of pictures; anything special before the mortuary van arrives?'

Hayes shook his head, nonplussed by the apparently pointless attack. First impression was that the sitting room had been turned over but not violently, not the mindless havoc generally associated with a break-in. Upstairs might have been more desperately searched, though, if Tessa Cox was to be believed; her eccentric employer had had enough sense to keep her valuable stock safely stashed at her London premises. But cash? Didn't dealers usually keep a wad to hand from sheer business habit, he wondered? But Bartram was not the obvious venue for deals, was it? And Mrs Cox seemed insistent that the dead woman kept her professional life at a distance from her weekend retreat.

It must hinge on the type of gallery Lulu Starewska ran. An expensive Aladdin's cave, by the sound of it, a place frequented by specialists. Exotic stuff. Maybe the Star Gallery was a magnet for cranky collectors or, for all he knew, Hayes admitted, the sort of decoration to appeal to an international clientele, rare art objects claiming a fanatical following of rich buyers with ethnic leanings.

He sighed and, after a few desultory questions about the state of the rooms upstairs, decided to let the scene of crime officers, known as the SOCO team, finish their job.

He turned to go but caught Taylor's arm as the sergeant started back to the crime scene.

'Hey, just one thing. The bloody cat. Did you throw it out?'

'Cat? Saw no cat, sir. You say there was a cat here?'

'It was in the kitchen when we arrived.

Gone, you say?'

Taylor shrugged, at a loss to understand the inspector's priorities. He stifled a grin. 'Never had you down as an animal lover, sir.'

Hayes frowned. 'It couldn't have gone far. If any of your lads spots it, let me know. It was sprayed with acid, it might be important. I'll get my men started on house-to-house enquiries. Someone must have seen *something* last night. A village like this is all eyes, any stranger would be noticed if only from behind the twitch of a curtain. And if we can't land our hands on a weapon, I might have to drag the bloody duck pond, God help me.'

Five

Hayes stepped outside just as DC Robbins was helping Tessa Cox into a police car. He waved her off, confident of Jenny Robbins' knack with traumatized witnesses. If there was something the woman was keeping to herself, the 'innocent curiosity' of a lowly constable would winkle it out. Eager to escape the horrific scene, Tessa Cox would find a sympathetic ear less daunting than the official enquiries of a chief inspector.

Hayes had worked with Jenny Robbins before and admitted that the girl had a special way with reluctant witnesses. Being young and pretty helped, of course. Those sherry-coloured eyes invited confidences, though Hayes was under no illusion that Tessa Cox was any pushover. Even in the course of a brief interview there was no mistaking a strong presence there. But why was she so anxious to see Lulu Starewska this afternoon? Keen enough to jog more than two miles in a storm after her car had broken down? Why not wait for assistance? Was there an urgency to warn the old woman? Had Tessa Cox information about a threat? A threat so great that she had rushed over to Bartram on foot?

He pushed these unanswerable questions to the back of his mind and collared his detective sergeant, Roy Bellamy, who was pulling in to the last available parking space on the edge of the Green. The wind had lifted, a storm-racked sky now settled into a sultry twilight. The few street lights around the Green cast an eerie glow over the jam of police cars and residents' vehicles crowding the narrow lane circling the grassy area and the duck pond. Hayes waited for his sergeant to emerge, his impatience all but visibly sparking.

'Bloody hell, Bellamy, where've you been? The SOCO team is practically finished.'

Bellamy scrambled out, his normally stolid features creased with anxiety. 'I was investigating a break-in on the industrial estate, sir. Mike Preston's message caught me on the hop. I had to complete the statements, haul the manager over to the site – you know what Sunday call-outs are like and—'

'Yeah, yeah. Well, now you're here you'd better liaise with Preston, organize a house-to-house. Mike'll fill you in. We'll have to move fast before the locals go off to work in the morning. The old lady was killed last night, before midnight. We shall need to know of any movements on this side of the Green on Saturday night. Set up your team and we'll have a briefing at eight thirty in the morning, by which time I shall expect you and Preston to have a summary of any useful statements. Now, clear off, you've wasted enough time already.'

Hayes moved purposefully back to Dolly Froude's cottage and knocked on the door. No time like the present when it came to nosy neighbours.

She ushered him in without a word, her composure, since the departure of Tessa Cox, settling.

'Come through, inspector. I was just pouring myself a stiff drink. May I tempt you?'

Hayes smiled, lighting up his aquiline features with an unexpected warmth that dispelled Dolly's reservations at a stroke. He was, she decided as she stood by the fire with a generous tot of post-traumatic stress buster in her hand, not such a stiffy after all.

'Thanks, Miss Froude, but no. May I sit?'
'Yes, of course.'
'I'm waiting for the forensics team to finish up but I hoped to have a quiet talk

with you now Mrs Cox has gone home. You knew her before?'

'Tessa? Oh yes. Clever girl. I've known Tessa since she was a kid. Her dad was my tutor at Oxford.'

'Ah yes. She mentioned being brought up in the area. Trimmingham, wasn't it? Her father taught at the university?'

She nodded. 'Charming man. An engineer, of course. Tessa's artistic bent came as a great surprise. She took a chemistry degree but later trained in art restoration and got a PhD from the conservation department of the Courtauld Institute. Her father was rather disappointed in the 'U turn' as he called it. He fancied his only child in line for a Nobel Prize,' she added with a loud guffaw. 'It was brave of Tessa to defy him. Professor Meakins must have been a formidable parent; though, as a tutor, I found him enormously encouraging.'

'You are an engineer?'

'Civil engineering. I travel a lot for my work. This cottage is my home base – Lulu and I were birds of passage, you might say.'

'Tell me about Mrs Starewska. She *was* "Mrs", I take it,' he said with a sly grin.

'Absolutely. Though God knows who the unlucky man was. She never spoke about a husband. I assumed she was a widow and we skirted round any touchy sexual relationships. My partner, Joyce Panton, lived here with me for twenty-two years. Died last December. Breast cancer, poor darling.' Dolly took a swig of whisky, her eyes misting over. 'Joyce kept house here when I was away on a job and Lulu and she were friends. Lulu had no hang-ups about us two women being "an item", as the Americans euphemistically call it.'

'Your partner was on familiar terms with Mrs Starewska?'

She laughed. 'Well, as familiar as Lulu wanted to be. She was a prickly customer, inspector, a very private person, especially about her business affairs. I introduced her to Tessa, you know. Lulu mentioned to Joyce that she was looking for a first-class conservator and I suggested Tessa. We met here for supper and Lulu took an instant shine to the girl. Tessa was working on a freelance basis like me, picked and chose her jobs as she could afford to do, not like poor old me, grabbing at any contract that came along.'

'She was living with her parents?'

'Not when she first started working for Lulu. Her father had retired early to care for his wife, who was failing fast at that time. She died quite suddenly in the end and

Tessa came home to be with him but he was a broken man. Professor Meakins passed away within a month of his wife, poor devil. Tessa gave up her London flat and has been here ever since. Works from home.'

'And her husband? Mr Cox?'

Dolly frowned, sipping her whisky, choosing her words with deliberation. 'Tessa deserved better, not that I'm the best judge of blokes, but Tony Cox was always a chancer. She married him on the rebound, if you ask me, in shock after her parents died. Lulu took to him, though. Funny that. She was a perceptive old bird, I would never have thought her to be taken in by a flash harry like Tony Cox. He's a car dealer, wouldn't you know? Classic job for a rogue,' she said with a glitter of malice. 'They moved into the farm at Trimmingham after the wedding and Lulu set him up with an outlet in Moscow. Star Motors. Sells luxury motors to Russian entrepreneurs, nothing but the best. Tony says the first thing these guys have on their shopping list once they've made their roubles is a Rolls or a Merc. Lulu encouraged him, I think he made her laugh. He is such a load of baloney, but they got on like a house on fire and, of course, Lulu was right. Despite being amused by Tony Cox, she was no fool;

helping to finance Star Motors was a shrewd move – it's been such a success he's opened a branch in St Petersburg. Fancy that! And, of course, Lulu has had contacts in Russia since for ever. How else do you think she stocks that gallery of hers?'

'How did you know that Mrs Starewska helped Cox to set up his business in Russia?'

'Oh, she mentioned it to Joyce; quite unlike Lulu to discuss her affairs but they had a little supper together while I was away on a job in Pakistan and I gather that the wine was flowing and at a guess I think Joyce was regarded as just a silly old spinster, of no possible threat in a commercial sense. Joyce was enormously discreet – except with me, of course – and the fact that we were instrumental in introducing Lulu to Tessa and her husband gave us a mutual interest, I suppose. Lulu seemed not to have any close friends, and I think the empathy between Joyce and herself was a comfort away from the cut and thrust of trading in antiques. Lulu was an old woman, inspector, despite her furious denials, and I think the gallery was secretly becoming something of a burden. Perhaps she was thinking of retiring, leaving that French manager of hers to take the weight off.'

Hayes played it dumb, hoping Dolly

Froude would come up with some useful information eventually. But she eyed him under lowered brows, assessing his bland responses with a smile, and changed the subject. 'I'll take Pushkin if you like.'

'Pushkin?'

'The cat. Lulu's cat. You said it needed looking after.'

Hayes got to his feet. 'Yes, sure. I've got my men on the lookout. It's gone AWOL but I'm sure if you call it it'll turn up. It knows you, I'm sure.'

'Oh, yes. Pushkin and I are old friends.'

Six

Roger Hayes cancelled his date with Pippa that evening; a night out at the Wigmore Hall, the debut of one of Roger's contemporaries, Franz Bulgari, a fellow student who had stuck at his studies and gained a piano scholarship at the Juilliard. The tickets had been a mixed blessing, complementaries sent by Franz's British agent, alerted by his protégé's aside that 'One of my friends at the Royal School is a senior policeman now.'

'He gave up?'

Franz had nodded, confirming his agent's belief that only the very best, the ones with vision, stuck out on the long road pitted with disappointments and sheer hard graft. But a policeman? A potential concert pianist pounding the beat? He had shrugged, privately noting that a friend in the Force was never a bad thing, and posted a couple of freebies to Hayes' base.

Pippa Cooper was not altogether surprised that the London trip had been cancelled. She imagined seeing Franz up there on the concert platform would have been a bitter pill despite Hayes' rapid climb up the police ladder. Hayes agreed to meet her later at her place.

He arrived late but in a surprisingly good mood, and toting a Chinese takeaway as a measly token of remorse. She drew him inside, smiling at this pretence that the recital had been the high spot of their plans for the weekend. Later they lay on the sofa, cosy by the fire, the coffee table strewn with empty cartons and half-filled wine glasses. Pippa wore a weird combination of jogging pants and a patchwork jacket, her eyes alert as a jackdaw's.

'You didn't really want to go, did you, darling?'

'Of course I did! Apart from occasional postcards and a backstage natter at the Young Musician of the Year final after I flunked out to begin my illustrious career as a super sleuth, I've not been in touch for years. Franz had a flashy technique as a kid, probably ironed out at the Juilliard.'

Pippa grimaced, unconvinced by this suave reposte. 'Actually,' she said, deftly changing the subject, 'I was a fan of your victim, Madame Starewska.'

'Really?'

'If you weren't such a philistine you'd have seen her yourself on BBC 4, that arts programme, *Spectrum*. I love it. Specializes in poisonous old farts rubbishing the latest exhibitions. Lulu could be an absolute witch. They wheeled her out with critics of the RA Summer Show or Tate Modern's latest blockbuster exhibit.'

Hayes sat up, suddenly alert. 'She wasn't ga-ga, then? You saw her recently?'

Pippa nodded, sipping her wine, watching him light a cigarette with affected nonchalance.

'She's got this marvellous gallery off Vicarage Road. I took a detour to check it out at Easter after seeing her demolish a Brit Art exhibition on telly. Wonderful place, dark as a cavern, lit only with huge shaded lamps and discreet spotlights trained on fabulous tapestries and gilt-framed mirrors. I couldn't afford so much as a thimble, of course, and I was stupid enough to think she'd be there at the till, serving the customers like it was a Tesco's checkout. Her manager was there all right, an oily bastard but terribly polite, probably guessed as soon as my scruffy trainers crossed the doormat that I was never a big spender.'

'She wore a wig, you know,' Roger put in,

relaxing behind a fog of cigarette smoke.

'Well, of course she bloody did. Genuine red hair like that only comes with bouncy constables like Jenny Robbins, and an old lady would never have enough hair of her own for a dye job. Poor old thing knew she wasn't fooling anyone, it was part of the image, her extraordinary style. I bet she was never a redhead, just fancied something outrageous to compliment her ghastly outfits. She sold stuff to Nureyev, you know. Kitted out his apartment in Paris when he couldn't go back to Russia.'

Hayes glanced at his watch. 'I've got to go, some notes to cook up before tomorrow's briefing.' He rose and reached for his coat.

Pippa's eyes widened. 'I hoped you'd stay.'

He kissed the top of her head and rattled his car keys in her ear. 'Not tonight, Josephine.'

'Actually,' she said, grabbing his sleeve, 'I forgot to mention that Best Boy is leaving at the end of the month.'

'Your lodger?'

'Got himself a job with the Outside Broadcasts Unit in Bristol.'

Hayes pulled a scarf from his pocket. 'Yeah, right.'

She sprang up. 'Why don't you move in, Rog? You're here most of the time anyway.'

He laughed unconvincingly, gently pulling away. 'What? And give up that crummy flat over the butcher's shop?' He grinned. 'Seriously, sweetheart, you'd hate it: out all hours, clarting up your bath with nasty pubic hairs down the plug-hole, moody as hell. You should talk to that ex-wife of mine, she walked out on all that.'

She pulled him close. 'You're not still beating yourself up over that, are you? I'm serious, Roger, think it over. There's no deadline.'

He drew away and quickly crossed to the door, blowing a kiss at the smiling girl silhouetted in the firelight. Pippa was right; there was no rush.

Next morning he arrived at the station prepped for the CID meeting. To his surprise his detective superintendent was waiting for him, impatiently pacing the reception area, causing the duty sergeant to bury his head in the rota sheets like a hedgehog hunkering down in a compost heap.

'Good. You're here, Hayes. Come to my office, I want a full run-down of progress before you brief the team.'

'Yes, sir. Lead on.'

Waller was a heavy man, thick shoulder muscles flexing uncomfortably within his wrinkled suit jacket, an air of latent irritability hanging around him like smog. Waller hated working with Hayes on a case like this. Their methods were diametrically opposed, Waller harbouring the suspicion that this po-faced chief inspector he had been stuck with was keeping him in the dark, leaving a nasty void into which he, cast as the lumbering bloody detective of the old school in Hayes' eyes, was likely to fall, only to clamber back on board with egg on his face.

They stiffly settled in his boss's superior room with its mahogany desk and dingy bookshelves. 'Well, come out with it, man. What leads have we got?'

Hayes shrugged. 'None, sir. Absolutely none.'

Seven

As soon as the briefing was concluded and Hayes had tossed Sergeant Preston back to the dragnet circling Bartram village, he called Jenny Robbins into his office, where she waited while he phoned the pathologist.

He concluded the call and glanced at his detective constable, outlined against the bleak north light of the window overlooking the market square. She wore jeans and a yellow polo-neck, her red-gold hair caught up in a ponytail, her slim figure tense as a greyhound in the slips.

'The pathologist is starting the autopsy at ten – I shall have to attend. I'll take Bellamy. Before I go, give me the lowdown on Mrs Cox. Anything interesting?'

She pulled a notebook from her pocket and stepped forward but before she could start, he pointed to a chair. 'For heaven's sake, sit down. All that pent-up energy makes me nervous.'

She took a seat and set off in an unstoppable stream of jumbled facts in the eager style he remembered all too well. Hayes picked the bones from her report like a fussy eater.

'Well, sir,' she continued, 'Mrs Cox was pretty quiet at first. And no wonder; all that blood! And an old lady too. Quite turned my stomach when she mentioned the acid touch and then—'

Hayes stiffened. 'She told you about the burns?'

Her hazel eyes narrowed. 'Yes, of course. She was the one who found the body, wasn't she?'

'She told me she only glanced at it before ringing 999. Did Mrs Cox confirm that Starewska's phone was off the hook?'

'She didn't say. She used her mobile.'

'Right. Go on.'

'I drove her back to Whipps Wood to check on her car. It was where she said. I checked. It *had* conked out. I asked her why she hadn't called the AA to get help but she said she wasn't a member. Her husband's a motor mechanic, he always checked their cars himself.'

'You left it there?'

'Of course. Mrs Cox said she had another car at home and that she'd get a local man to pick it up today.'

'Did she say why she was in such a hurry to see Lulu Starewska?'

'All she admitted was that it was a business matter, something she needed to confirm before the old woman went back to London. I tried to get more detail but she clammed up.'

'Did she speak about her relationship with the victim?'

'Only to say they sometimes disagreed about the extent of treatment that was required. Mrs Cox is a stickler for the authentic and she admitted that Starewska often wanted a cosmetic job on a painting, which, as a conservator, she found unacceptable.'

'They quarrelled?'

'I don't think so. Just two determined characters with a different agenda. The gallery needed attractive stuff that would appeal to a buyer and Mrs Cox had academic scruples, especially when handling the icons.'

'Icons? Isn't there a ban on importing icons?'

She shrugged. 'Search me. Anyway, by the time we got to her house, she was quite excited about all this and rambled on about her repair work. Right over my head, of course, but I played along and she invited me to see her studio.'

'Recovered from the shock damn quick then?'

'Mm. I suppose she had, now I come to think about it, but you know what these workaholics are like once they get into their subject.'

Hayes laughed. 'Yeah. Well, cut the crap, Robbins. Anything else?'

'Well, this so-called farm is no smallholding, sir. More like a manor house. Old. Part Tudor, all gables and stuff, with a converted barn accommodating this studio of hers. We went straight into the workshop from a side entrance but it was well secured, burglar alarm, blinds down at the windows and a CCTV over the entrance.'

Hayes impatiently nodded. 'Crack on, kiddo, I've got to be at the mortuary in half an hour.'

'It was more like a lab than a studio. You've never seen so much scientific equipment; scanner, micro cameras you could do keyhole surgery with, but not a single artwork in sight.'

'Locked away?'

'I asked but she was evasive. Said she used a safe and changed the subject. Started burbling on about her husband being abroad. I suggested she got a friend or someone to stay but she said her stepson was due back from a school skiing trip at the end of the week and she had a pile of work on hand before he got back. He's only nine – probably needs a lot of attention, as little boys do.'

'Stepson?'

'Her husband's child from a previous marriage. Tony Cox got sole custody three years ago after his ex-wife was considered unfit by the authorities.'

'Unfit? In what way?'

'She didn't elaborate, thanked me for the lift and tried to bundle me out damn quick. It was if it had occurred to her that she'd said too much but, frankly, I couldn't work it out. To make it official I asked if she felt able to present herself here this morning to make a statement.'

'Good. We also need a set of fingerprints for elimination purposes. You'd better ring her and arrange a time; she's used to you and won't make a fuss. Doesn't need transport, you say? Another car at home?'

'And how! I spotted a Merc and a Jeep tucked away at the side but if her husband's in the car business that's not surprising, is it? Bad luck choosing the one that broke down in a rainstorm, though. It wasn't her day, was it, sir?' she added with a grin.

Hayes stood and shuffled some papers into his briefcase. 'I don't suppose Mrs Cox said anything about the deceased? Mentioned relatives? Next of kin?'

She shook her head, the ponytail dancing. 'I tried that tack but she closed up. Denies knowing any personal information about Mrs Starewska. One interesting thing, though, sir. A reporter stopped me at the gate, the arts correspondent of one of the broadsheets, *The Times* or the *Telegraph*, I forget which.'

Hayes bridled. 'I've told you a million times, Robbins, never, on any account, talk to the press.'

She stood her ground, the amber eyes gleaming dangerously. 'Yes, sir. But this chap, Mark Morrison, said he was a friend, making a personal call on Tessa Cox, offering condolences, I suppose. He knew about her collaboration with Starewska and got a flash from his editor about Cox finding the body. There's going to be an obituary in the paper this week, a full biographical piece about the old lady, and Morrison mentioned the name of the man who is writing it up. An art historian called Professor Stenning. I asked for an intro and he offered to take us to meet him. The professor is based in Oxford, hardly a detour, sir.' She extracted a business card from her notebook and passed it over. 'Morrison jotted down the professor's college on the back of his card and I said I'd be in touch. I thought it might be useful, sir; a source of information about Mrs Starewska's background, a lead to any surviving next-of-kin, perhaps?' She smiled, a barely disguised smirk of vindication.

Hayes stared at the card and then passed it back. 'I've more sense than get involved with the press, Robbins. You deal with it. Track down this Professor Whatsisname and sift through anything useful. If necessary, go with this journalist, Morrison but, for Christ's sake, don't give him anything about the crime scene. If anyone's giving press interviews, Superintendent Waller's the man for the job. After I've got some facts from the pathologist, I'm driving down to London to speak to the manager of the gallery. Sergeant Bellamy's fixing it up. Call me on my mobile if anything interesting turns up via Morrison and keep Mrs Cox sweet. I'm convinced she's holding out on us.'

Jenny Robbins followed him out, making a beeline for an empty desk to make her phone calls. Hayes' detective sergeant, Roy Bellamy, waited patiently for his boss to emerge from the extended tête-à-tête with the pert young constable dubbed Robin Redbreast in the canteen, her enthusiasm earning her an ungenerous ration of veiled hostility. This girl was clearly destined for promotion and as such was treated with kid gloves by the rest of the team.

It was rumoured that Jenny Robbins had, in fact, introduced Hayes to his current girlfriend, Pippa Cooper, when she had lodged in Cooper's cottage. Hayes stiffly retained a professional stance towards their pretty constable but there was no denying that Jenny Robbins was often included in investigations that would normally be shared by a more senior officer. She had a knack with witnesses and had enjoyed a notable success with a recent murder case for which Hayes had got the credit, but the CID squad remained cautious when the usual teasing of the junior ranks, especially the WPCs, would normally include Jenny Robbins. DS Bellamy remained sanguine. The girl would soon be promoted and, with luck, transferred.

Eight

Sergeant Bellamy drove Hayes to London, the silence only interrupted by terse questions about the house-to-house enquiries in Bartram. Local response had been enthusiastic, the old lady's violent death being a source of horror, especially to the elderly residents who knew Lulu Starewska by sight if not on any basis of familiarity. But useful information was elusive, the bad weather combined with a televised international football match driving most of the residents to stay at home.

'There are no buses on Sundays, sir. But there was a general moan about the kids using the bus shelter outside Star Cottage as a meeting point, especially at weekends. Ghetto blasters were the usual cause of complaint and on one occasion a few weeks ago these lads had a Hallowe'en party with fireworks that set the wooden shelter alight and burned the place down. After that the council replaced it with a metal structure without bench seats, which seems to have solved the problem, which is bad news for us. If the kids had been partying in the bus shelter on Saturday night we might have had some useful witnesses.'

'Did you find out if Starewska was one of those complaining to the council about the use of the shelter?'

'I asked Mike Preston to talk to the vicar about it as he was the guy co-ordinating the complaints. Oddly enough, the old lady was vehemently against the council's decision to take out the seats. She wrote a strong letter to the chairman, berating them for providing no alternative venue where the youngsters could meet.'

'Starewska didn't mind the racket right outside her front door?'

'Not at all. She was away the night of the fire. It could have set alight her thatched roof and she might have taken a different view, but the blaze happened midweek and by the time she heard about it the damage had been cleared away. Mind you, sir, Preston got the impression from the vicar that she was one of those who had a running battle with the church *and* the council, so putting herself on the side of the yobs could have just been cussedness. But it's true, there's nothing in the village for teenagers;

no youth club or anything.'

'I guess Mrs Starewska was awkward by nature,' Hayes dryly remarked. 'Did anyone make a list of the lads who regularly used the bus shelter?'

'No, but the vicar would oblige, he was the one organizing the petition to remove the benches.'

'Get their names and addresses, will you? They probably know more about who was in and out of that cottage than the neighbours.'

The car crawled through the afternoon city traffic as they passed the Hogarth roundabout and approached the vicinity of the gallery.

'He is expecting us, the manager?'

'Yes, sir. His name's Raoul Musset. Has worked for Mrs Starewska for years, so he said. Seemed quite cut up.'

'Worried about his career prospects, poor devil.'

Bellamy made a swift left turn and cut through a series of back doubles that brought them to the gallery entrance. Velvet curtains were drawn across the shop window and a steel grille that, augmented by a 'Closed' notice on the door, shut off any promise of trading. Hayes rapped on the glass and in seconds a face peered out from behind the grille. Several locks rasped as the entrance was unbarred and a short, dapper man wearing a tight brocade waistcoat ushered them quickly inside as if they might be KGB men with dangerous questions.

The shop was dimly lit, silver reflections flickering in the darkness from a selection of mirrors and a gleaming samovar. An exotic scent hung like incense, the walls draped with tapestries, the atmosphere as alien as a Russian church.

Hayes smiled, imagining Pippa bouncing into the gallery anticipating a welcoming salesman's pitch, which would have been a very unlikely response from the man standing anxiously to one side to guide them into the back room. Hayes introduced himself and showed his ID card.

The manager bowed. 'Raoul Musset, sir. How may I help you?'

The office was cluttered; a computer, TV and video machine, a bank of filing cabinets, and an exceptionally large rosewood desk almost filling the small room. Two spindly gilt chairs were pulled up to the desk and the manager settled himself into an ornate throne-like chair, which seemed only to rob him of any stature. Musset was distinctly nervous, his eyes darting from Hayes to Bellamy in anxious anticipation of some sort of grilling. Hayes wondered if Monsieur Musset had had a bad experience of police methods.

'Now, sir, shall we make this as brief as possible? Your employer – I take it Mrs Starewska *was* in control here? – died in what we policeman term "suspicious circumstances" and we have very little background information. Before we proceed, would you like to ask any questions?'

This invitation was a mistake. Raoul Musset cleared his throat and, gripping the edge of the desk, broke into a fusillade of accented English that grew more garbled as the words spewed out. Hayes attempted to interrupt with no success.

'Madame was my friend, my dearest friend,' he insisted. 'We have worked together for sixteen years and although I must admit Madame's style was often – how do you say? – acerbic? – we had a deep love for the things you see here in the gallery. My lady had perfect taste and an unwavering eye for the authentic, and so naturally the Star Gallery enjoyed the regard of collectors and dealers the world over.'

Breaking the flow at last, Hayes curtly cut in. 'Mrs Starewska also attracted a certain animosity, I believe? Among experts?'

'Envy! Pure envy. Madame was a fearless

warrior for our art and promoted East European and Asian treasures despite the catcalls. As a result of the fall of the Soviet empire, classic artworks appeared in the West for the first time in generations and our little enterprise catered for an increasing interest in the style. Naturally, our most loyal clients are those exiled here or preferring to live in the West, but one or two interior decorators have recognized the potential and I need hardly add that a steady influx of Russian émigrés of millionaire status has been a bonus. The demand has almost become a flood, chief inspector.'

Bellamy had attempted to make a note of Musset's outpourings but, defeated by the increasingly accented delivery, now gave up and sat, slack jawed, waiting for Hayes to pull the interview together.

'Yes, indeed, but my biggest problem, Mr Musset, is compiling a profile of Mrs Starewska's life.'

'Madame died in a terrible, terrible attack, I understand from the news. Knifed in her own home...' Musset's voice trailed into a whisper and beads of sweat shone on his upper lip, Pippa's description of the man as 'an oily bastard' now seeming at odds with the unfortunate soul slumped at the desk.

'Next of kin, Mr Musset? Did Mrs Stare-wska have any family?'

'No, none at all.'

'Abroad perhaps?'

'Madame's marriage was brief, the union childless. Arriving in London as a refugee, she was alone and penniless, and made her life's work here in this gallery, bringing our treasures to the attention of an art world that is only now appreciating the beauty of what you can see around you.' He wafted a ringed hand towards several icons hanging along a back wall. 'These are too precious to have on general display. Fourteenth- and fifteenth-century pieces, holy objects to be revered.'

Hayes eyes narrowed as he focussed on the jewel-like paintings, his mind assessing the possible value of such exotic exhibits.

'You have access to these "holy objects", Mr Musset? An agent in Greece or Russia?'

'We deal only in Russian icons. Mrs Starewska employs an expert who tours the villages, seeking out purchases. You must understand that after the revolution churches were closed and many religious artefacts neglected or even destroyed. It is only in recent years that the orthodox church has been free, but salvaging icons is a delicate business. Some were kept secretly in attics by peasants loyal to their heritage but many, many thousands were used for firewood or abused. Our agent, Dmitri, has to tread carefully, tracing treasured church items often covertly passed down though families only to re-emerge if the church is rebuilt. Such things are regarded as the property of the villagers and the purchase of even distressed artworks is a matter of lengthy negotiation, the actual ownership being unclear.'

Bellamy shifted uncomfortably on his gilt chair and glanced at his watch, wondering how much time Hayes was prepared to waste listening to all this. But Hayes seemed fascinated.

'And you can bring these things here without exit permits?'

Musset glanced down at the blotter, his eyes hooded. 'Oh yes. The market is new at present. And most reclaimed artworks are in such a poor state of repair that only an expert could discern their barest outline.'

'And that is were Mrs Cox came in, I suppose?'

Musset shuffled his feet, ruffling the silk rug beneath the desk, and regarded Hayes with bloodshot eyes. 'Ah yes, Mrs Cox. A useful discovery of Madame's. Mrs Cox cleaned pictures for us to make them saleable.'

Hayes pulled himself together, shaking off the picture Raoul Musset's diatribe had put in mind. Peasants squirreling away valuable art? Filthy, unrecognizable icons travelling from farm attics in a remote Russian province to reappear in a London gallery?

'Very interesting, sir. But to get back to procedure. In the absence of any next of kin would you be prepared to come to Oxford to identify the body?'

Musset rose, his features wreathed in smiles. 'But of course, chief inspector. The gallery will remain closed until after Madame's funeral. I am entirely at your disposal.'

Hayes got to his feet and after a short discussion settled on an appointment at the mortuary the following day. Musset ushered them through the 'shop', as Bellamy obstinately regarded it, but, as they waited while Starewska's manager fumbled with the locks and chains of the front entrance, Hayes put in a parting shot.

'You must be anxious about your situation since your employer's sudden death?'

The 'oily bastard' persona re-established itself as Raoul Musset drew to his full height, seeming visibly to grow in stature, his lips parting in a discreet smile. 'Not at all, my dear sir. Madame was kind enough to promise that after her death – she was after all in her declining years – I would be entirely in control of the Star Gallery. I have an appointment with the solicitor on Thursday. *Everything* has been promised to Raoul Alban Musset, including her apartment in St Bede's Square.'

Hayes tensed. 'In that case, Mr Musset, you will have no objection to our inspection of Mrs Starewska's flat? The keys were unaccountably missing from the cottage.'

Musset's reply hardly missed a beat. 'But, of course. If you will kindly wait a moment I will give you the spare keys from the office.' He hurried off, leaving the two men on the doorstep, and quickly returned, handing Hayes a bundle of keys. 'It would be sensible until probate is secured that the keys are returned to Madame's solicitor in due course.' He handed a lawyer's business card to Bellamy, who was attempting to scribble a receipt for the keys. This small parting performance concluded with hands shaken all round and the door closed with finality.

Bellamy was visibly narked. 'I thought you would ask him where *he* was on Saturday night, sir. Sounds as if he had plenty of opportunity to hurry along his promotion to sole proprietor.'

'Tomorrow, Bellamy. Once he's in shock after seeing the poor victim on the mortuary slab, I've got several questions to put to our friend. Let's drive over to this place of hers and have a good look round while we're on the spot.'

Bellamy unlocked the car and they picked their way across the royal borough to Lulu Starewska's London home.

Nine

Jenny Robbins agreed to meet Mark Morrison in a basement coffee bar on the High. The weather had not improved and she hurried along the busy pavement, shielding herself from a gusty wind with her umbrella. Just as she reached the basement steps the brolly blew inside out, sending a cascade of droplets down the neck of her ski jacket.

The place was warm and brightly lit, and decked with plastic holly garlands and silk poinsettias. The weeks before Christmas were the best of it, she decided, the heady atmosphere of students in a persistent party mood augmented by the scent of pine needles trodden underfoot in those few shops that favoured authentic décor proving a perennial surprise.

She tossed the broken umbrella under a crush of coats gently steaming on a rack by the door and looked around for her contact.

He rose from a seat by the window, waving his newspaper, and she picked her way between the crowded tables to join him. 'I ordered an Americano for you. OK? We don't want to hang about. The professor's expecting us at noon.'

Jenny nodded and flopped into the empty seat, smiling a full octane grin that made Mark Morrison's pulse miss a beat. Her damp hair had escaped to frame her forehead in wispy ringlets. Very Botticelli.

'It's good of you to go to all this trouble,' she said. 'Was the professor happy to talk to me about Mrs Starewska?'

'Absolutely delighted. Keen to put his view of the poor lady. He says too many people were rude about her when, in fact, she was first on the scene to promote East European art. It paid off handsomely in the long run, of course, but Lulu Starewska put up with a load of flak before the Berlin wall came down and access was more freely available.'

Jenny sugared her coffee and focussed on her informant. Hayes' dislike of the press made her position delicate but, with no leads as to who hated the victim enough to mount such a vicious attack, there seemed no point in being prissy.

'Tell me,' she whispered, 'about Tessa Cox.'

Mark Morrison was no fashion victim for

sure. His leather jacket was missing two buttons and the emerging cuff of a baggy sweater was unravelling into a ragged frill. In other respects he was, she had to admit, more than personable. Thirtyish. Intelligent grey eyes behind narrow spectacles focussing on her with keen interest. And, the thing she liked most; no designer stubble, an affectation she found oddly unattractive. Perhaps she had got too familiar with the clean-cut style of Hayes' team?

Mark lit a cigarette and paused before answering.

'Actually, I was seriously smitten with Tessa when we were both at the Courtauld. She wasn't most guys' choice; too clever, too snooty, too rich. But we linked up for a whole year, even shared notes – in those days my work ethic was easily shipwrecked. But falling in love was not on Tessa's agenda. Very single-minded, utterly committed, determined to prove to her father that she was serious, I guess.'

'You lost touch?'

'Not entirely. I wanted to write and bagged a job as a hack on *Gallery* magazine, but Tessa needed to tend the sacred flame, concentrate on academic research. And being in no way short of funds, she was free to work only on the things that interested her.'

'Seriously rich or just well off?'

'Oh no. Wealthy. Her father was an Oxford man but from the Waites' tobacco family, and her mother was not exactly lacking a dowry by all accounts. Tessa had a chemistry degree before she took up art conservation, which gave her the edge over the rest of us.'

'But not popular with her fellow students?'

'Gave the impression of superciliousness but was really just shy. I got lucky. Persistence always pays off,' he added with a brittle laugh.

'Didn't add up to any lasting romance, though?'

'Not really. An off and on affair until her mother died and after that she was bowled over by bloody Tony Cox who, bitter as I might sound, was really the last sort in my mind to appeal to an intelligent girl like Tessa.' He glanced at his watch and finished his coffee. 'Let's go. We can walk from here. We don't want to be late, these Oxford dons hate to miss their lunch.'

Jenny threw on her jacket and they left in a hurry, bowling down the street against the strong wind, clutching each other like a pair of drunks.

Professor Stenning's rooms were as snug

as any elderly academic could possibly wish; book-lined walls and a Persian carpet cosied a pad with only the overlying fug of cigarette smoke and sweet sherry for students to gag on. The professor was short and balding with tufts of grey at his temples, giving the old man a passing resemblance to an eaglet.

'Come in, come in, young people. Make yourselves comfortable. A glass of wine?'

'Not for me, thank you, sir,' Morrison said, introducing Jenny, who sat demurely on the scuffed leather sofa, hoping she looked a harmless enough detective.

The professor plumped for a swivel chair, his feet doing a quick shuffle as he turned to face them. 'You are interested in my dear friend Lulu Starewska, young lady?'

'We are anxious to catch the person who did this, Professor Stenning, and anything you can give us will be enormously helpful. The police have been unable to trace any relatives. Her personal life is a bit of a mystery.'

Stenning selected a cigarette, fastidiously inserting it into an ivory holder and taking his time with a box of matches. The room was instantly scented with an odd fragrance Jenny could only surmise to be Turkish.

'Personal life? In that respect I fear the page is almost blank. However, the dear lady and I had been friends for years, since the early fifties at any rate, a period of enormous excitement for us as the auction rooms were trading in masterworks once again and the public was becoming familiar with the treasures that had remained hidden during the war years. Lulu and I were working on an international enquiry to trace artworks stolen during the war. We were,' he said, pausing to blow a smoke ring, 'hardly successful, but the work goes on still and we hope our contribution was worthwhile. Lulu's contacts with an underworld of informants was invaluable. Her maiden name was Ludmilla Starewska but her date of birth is shrouded in the mists of time, as any respectable lady is entitled to decide. Lulu claimed to be sixty-five, which is arrant nonsense, of course. Her marriage to Dennison, a lowly diplomat, was brief and unverifiable. Took place in Paris so she said but none of us dared to question her about him, it was a subject completely off the record as far as my dear friend was concerned.'

'But she had British citizenship?'

'Oh yes. That was true enough.'

'But no children?' Mark interjected.

'Apparently not. But I do have some snapshots which may interest you, Morrison. Photographs of Lulu taken after the war. A lovely, lovely woman.'

He rose and shuffled through a sheaf of papers on his desk. Mark's eyes lit up. The pictures were, in fact, faded and hardly of studio quality, but there was no denying that Starewska had been a stunner. Several shots had been taken on a rocky shore, the bland features of a young Professor Stenning immediately recognizable, a man for whom the years had merely thickened the outline.

'In the sixties. A symposium jaunt on the Black Sea coast organized by the British Council. A group of us, mostly lecturers, made up a fascinating party. University people, of course, but Lulu came along as a specialist and brought a young friend, an undergraduate called Smyth, as I recall, that dark fellow there, see? A bit of a bounder, ended up doing three years for fraud.'

Mark lit a cigarette, the cheap smoke filtering the professor's superior brand like a cheeky interloper. 'Tell me, sir, when did Mrs Starewska open the gallery?'

Stenning made a small moue, his lips pursing childishly. 'Oh, good heavens, Morrison, the gallery was a halfway milestone; Lulu was buying and selling from home for years before that. She was a linguist, of course. French, Russian, Polish, and travelled everywhere with her agent. A man called

Dmitri, I can't recall any details. The gallery was established after a particularly success-ful coup. Lulu secured some eighteenth-century portraits allegedly acquired from a hoard hidden by White Russians living in Paris.'

'Allegedly?'

Stenning tapped ash into a silver bonbon dish. 'Her methods were mysterious, prob-ably her way of fixing the price. Lulu invited me to authenticate this group of paintings that were absolutely "right". After the sale – these beauties were snapped up by a Jap-anese collector, I heard – the Star Gallery was born.'

'Auctioned?'

'No. A private arrangement.' He laughed, a dry cackle that temporarily reduced the professor to a coughing fit. They waited and finally he recovered and continued, a smile puckering his eyes as he recalled his old friend. 'Lulu worked on contacts, always contacts. Opening the gallery was no more than a front. Important transactions were always under cover. That manager of hers was merely window dressing.'

'Is her agent still operating?'

'I've no idea. If Lulu owed him money you can be sure he'll be on the gallery doorstep pronto. Must be an old man himself now, a

Russian, I believe, a former Cossack according to Lulu but she was a wonderful enhancer of the facts. All I know is he got himself into serious trouble with the immigration people about a false visa and Lulu bailed him out. A kind woman. All heart. Sentimentally drawn to baddies, I fear, but inflexible when it came to a deal. If one is born in poverty, scraping along as a refugee with nothing but one's wits to save you, money can become an obsession. Lulu loved the treasures she claimed to have discovered in obscurity and brought into the light, but in her latter years money became her master, I am sorry to say. Nothing of this is of public interest, of course, my obituary is pure hagiography, but the fact remains Ludmilla Starewska was a comet in the art firmament.'

Mark Morrison kept the ball rolling smoothly but nothing helpful to the investigation seemed to emerge.

'Would you like a copy of the obituary, my dear? I faxed my piece to the paper this morning.'

Jenny nodded, jumping to her feet, eager to get back to Bartram, where she was likely missing all the action.

The professor slid some typewritten sheets into an envelope, and Mark continued a polite conversation as Jenny edged towards the door.

Outside, in the rain, he offered to give her a lift back to the park-and-ride. 'My car's in the college car park, just at the back here.'

'Actually mine's behind the police station near the coffee shop. I can walk.' Her tone was light but disappointment bloomed in the air like mildew.

'No joy then?'

'Well, the prof didn't have a lot to further our investigation, did he?' she snapped.

'The obit. might show up something fresh,' he put in, wondering if his lack of success on the female front was indicated by a watermark on his forehead. This detective constable was nice. He made a final shot.

'How about dinner one night? I'm based in London but there's some stuff I need to check out while I'm in Oxford.'

Jenny frowned. 'Actually, I'm on call pretty well full time while this murder is still priority. Can I ring you later? I've got your card.'

Mark smiled grimly but cheerfully shook hands, watching the slim figure peel off through the crowd of urgent shoppers. He shrugged and hurried into the nearest pub. Some Christmas cheer was called for.

Ten

Lulu Starewska's flat lay on the first floor of a two-storey building dominating St Bede's Square, a quiet garden square north of Oxford Street. They peered through the glazed doors at an empty lobby dominated by a counter and back office, presumably the caretaker's domain. The office was apparently unmanned and access through the main entrance was locked. Persistent ringing of the doorbell brought no response.

It was after five in the afternoon by the time Hayes and Sergeant Bellamy had arrived, and the car spaces were all occupied. A single lamp post offered sparse illumination and the darkness was deepened by trees overhanging the railings surrounding the development.

Hayes rang again but it seemed clear that no doorman was going to show up. Bellamy tried one of the keys Raoul Musset had passed over and they went inside.

'Not much in the way of security, sir,'

Bellamy observed, his gloomy appraisal of the scuffed marble foyer and the cranky lift failing to warm him to this art deco building and its musty, unlived-in atmosphere. 'Not so much as a CCTV by the front door. Wouldn't mind betting smoke alarms are well down on the management's priorities an'all.'

'The owners are probably waiting for the elderly leaseholders to kick the bucket so they can transform the units into expensive service flats. The location's excellent: within walking distance of the tube and a nice garden square to look out on.'

The lift wheezed to the next floor, where they were confronted with a very long corridor and a dozen front doors behind which a number of people, Hayes guessed mostly to be single occupants, lived in lonely seclusion.

Lulu Starewska's door was unremarkable, varnished with the same dark stain as its neighbours. Bellamy inserted a Yale key, then activated the mortice lock and the door swung open to reveal a narrow hallway. The light-bulb overhead was missing and, in the darkness, they groped their way through until Bellamy located a functioning switch in the sitting room. Hayes paused to assess the layout.

It was a tiny flat, comprising a kitchenette leading off the sitting room, a bedroom with two single beds, and a chipped avocado suite in the windowless bathroom. The curtains were drawn and the air fusty.

At first glance the place seemed neat but uncared for, the only comfortable chair pulled close to a gas fire, a bunch of dried flowers on a long coffee table as cheerless as a wreath on a coffin. No pictures, no books and only a portable television set to while away the empty hours.

Expecting an exotic interior in tune with the gallery, and bearing in mind Pippa's description of Starewska, Hayes was baffled. If this was what Lulu called 'home', it was barely a miserable pied-à-terre. Perhaps she had regarded her cottage at Bartram as her real home, a place to relax, whereas this anonymous bolt-hole had just been somewhere to lay her head at the end of a working day. The single homely touch was Pushkin's cat basket cosied up with a quilted cushion and occupying a prime spot next to the gas fire.

The lighting was dim, provided mainly by a lamp with a fringed silk shade, the overhead light also out of commission.

'The old lady didn't put light-bulbs top of her shopping list, eh, sir? That's the second one kaput.'

Hayes continued to gaze around, puzzled. 'I don't like this, Bellamy. It's too tidy. No dishes on the draining board, no muddle of books or pills on the old woman's bedside table, nothing out of place at all. I reckon someone's been in since Starewska went away for the weekend. Either a cleaner or a nosy caretaker.'

At that moment there was a furious banging at the front door. 'Open up! Police.'

Bellamy started up, his eyes on stalks. Hayes laughed, crossed to the hallway and opened the door. A gaunt female wearing a navy blazer and pleated skirt blocked the entrance, backed by a burly constable, plus a nervous old dear peeping from behind.

'And who the hell are you?' the woman barked.

'ID?' Hayes laconically requested.

She flashed her identity card and glowered. 'Inspector Bass to you,' she said, and pushed her way inside, leaving the constable and the old lady to man the exit.

'Snap!' countered Hayes, producing his own ID card. 'Chief Inspector Hayes to you,' he added with a grin. 'What's all this about then?'

She scowled and, turning on her heel, grabbed the woman sheltering behind the policeman and pulled her roughly inside, closing the door, leaving her backup on the doormat.

'This lady, Mrs Sharpley, rang to complain about intruders in her friend's flat. She lives next door.'

'The walls are very thin,' the trembling informant explained. 'I was worried. Lulu had no family, you see – I thought it was the burglars back.'

'Burglars *back?* You said nothing about any previous break-in, Mrs Sharpley,' Bass snapped.

She blanched, clearly overawed by the number of police officers her complaint had dragged to the scene.

'Well, you see, I am a light sleeper and on Sunday, about three o'clock in the morning, I woke to hear movements in Lulu's flat, and knowing she was away for the weekend I wondered if she had allowed Rory to stay over. Later, I began to get bothered in case it had been a thief but, by then, it was too late so I let it pass. But when I heard more noise in here this afternoon, and knowing that poor Lulu's death had been in all the papers, I thought I'd better call the police to check. One hears such dreadful things about burglars taking advantage when they know a place is empty.'

Hayes touched her arm and smiled. 'Quite right too, Mrs Sharpley. A good neighbour is rare these days.'

'I'll be off then,' Inspector Bass retorted, taking a step towards the door. 'Now that you are in charge here, chief inspector, we don't want too many cooks spoiling the broth, do we? I assume you are working on the murder investigation. As a matter of interest, how did you get in?'

'Keys,' Bellamy put in, dangling the chunky bunch of keys from one finger. 'Provided by Mrs Starewska's manager.'

'The beneficiary of her will. The keys will be returned to the late Mrs Starewska's solicitor in due course.'

Bass nodded and made to go but Hayes called her back. 'Hang about, inspector. What about this lady's statement? Mrs Sharpley heard intruders over the weekend. *Are* you investigating it?'

She paused, momentarily off balance, and turned to face the unfortunate neighbour. 'Do you wish to take this further, Mrs Sharpley?'

The old woman looked doubly confused, her rheumy eyes darting from Hayes to Bass. 'Well, if there was no burglary it must have been my imagination, mustn't it? This old building creaks terribly at night, the service manager says it's because the pipes need renewing.'

Hayes smiled. 'Perhaps we could talk again once my sergeant and I have made sure nothing is missing? You live next door? Number thirty-eight?'

She nodded and was all but frog-marched out by Bass. The door closed and the inspector returned to face Hayes. 'As a reported break-in has now been withdrawn, I shall take my leave, chief inspector.'

Hayes remained impassive. 'Actually I am still in two minds about that. I shall leave my sergeant here to secure the premises until I'm satisfied that no crime has been committed. Perhaps you should make a note of my precautions in your report.'

Bass sketched a thin smile before she walked out without another word, slamming the door.

Hayes grimaced. 'Ghastly creature, that Bass woman. Never fancied these stick insect types myself. Still, I haven't entirely discounted the old lady's story about hearing an intruder in here in the early hours on Sunday night. What do you think, Bellamy? If she's right, whoever it was let himself in with keys. And, for the record, Bellamy, no keys to Starewska's flat were found at the cottage. Our poor victim would never have gone down to the country without her house keys, would she? Let's have another look round and, with luck, I'll get Superintendent Waller to sanction a fingerprint search here. Don't touch anything but keep your eyes skinned. Whoever killed Starewska is the likely lad to have stolen her keys and continued his search here for whatever he couldn't find at the cottage.'

'We don't know there were only two sets of keys, do we, sir? Musset could have another set squirreled away and as the inheritor of the business he may have got impatient to see his boss off the scene.'

Hayes frowned. 'Yeah, sure, but who's this "Rory" Mrs Sharpley seemed to think was welcome to stay over? I wouldn't have thought Starewska was likely to offer a bed to a bloke, seeing as she had no family and was hardly, from all we hear, the sort to share her privacy. You stay here, Bellamy, until I can get the locks changed. Shouldn't take more than an hour and at least we'd know the place was not open house to our mysterious interloper. We need to get forensics to pull the place apart though, frankly, any intruder bright enough to leave everything tidy here isn't the sort to leave his fingerprints. Our SOCO team found precious little evidence at the cottage that we could use to identify the killer. Anyway, while you're here take a dekko through her desk, while I see what else Mrs Sharpley can tell us about this Rory character.'

Eleven

Mrs Sharpley's flat was as cosy as her late neighbour's was sparse. A sofa and chairs covered in sprigged linen promoted a summery feel to a sitting room warmed by an electric fire doing its best to pretend to be glowing coals, an invisible device lighting the fake fire with simulated ash.

She welcomed Hayes with a nervous smile. 'I've made some tea, inspector. If you're not too busy, won't you join me? I could do with some company, this afternoon's trouble has left me rather trembly.'

'Just the ticket, Mrs Sharpley. Milk and two sugars would be great. I'm waiting for some assistants to check next door. Nice place you've got here. Been here long?'

'Just four years. My son, Peter, managed to get a short lease for me, all I could afford in Central London, but I wanted to be near my grandchildren. They're at school just down the road so can sometimes pop in on their way home. Teenagers. Two lovely girls.

I'm very lucky.'

She fetched a cup for Hayes, who glanced round, impressed by the comfort the old lady had managed to produce in a flat identical to Starewska's. The furniture gleamed with wax, leaving a lingering scent of lavender, and a red poinsettia stood on the sideboard together with a bunch of Christmas cards.

'I lived in Devon before my husband died, but Peter persuaded me to sell up. Wanted me to move into an old people's residence but I'm not quite ready for that yet,' she said with a wobbly smile. 'This place is a sort of halfway house. I've made the best of it but Lulu's attack has hit me hard. Perhaps it is time to move on. What do you think, inspector?'

Hayes hardly considered himself a natural with old folk, his own parents long since passed away, but he felt an unexpected sympathy with this reluctant witness, whose genuine concern for her friend's property had been pushed aside in the crush of police reports in which no doubt Inspector Bass was snowed under.

'No need for you to worry, Mrs Sharpley. I'll have a word with the caretaker, see if we can persuade him to beef up the door-keeping. Mrs Starewska was attacked miles away

81

from here, probably a local criminal already on our books in Renham. We'll sort him out, it just takes time. Now, easy does it, just tell me exactly what you heard on Sunday night. I'm sure there's a simple explanation.'

She sipped her tea, mollified by the nice young man's pleasant manner.

'Nothing much to worry about, now I think back on it. Just shuffling about, drawers opening and closing, floorboards squeaking, that sort of thing.'

'And the time was?'

'Ten past three. I looked at my alarm clock. Whoever it was was keeping very quiet about it. That's what made me think when I woke up this morning that it must have been Rory. You found nothing missing? Nothing stolen? Lulu had some very important jewellery, you know. Amber necklaces, rows of them, and a lot of long earrings, nothing to tempt me but Lulu had a very dramatic style, all those colourful get-ups and beads really suited her. She was sometimes on the television, you know. I don't have those extra programmes my son talks about, just the regular channels, but I saw her on a discussion programme one evening when I was looking after my granddaughters.' She laughed, her faded blue eyes creasing with amusement. 'Lulu was being really outrageous – no shame at all.'

'But you were good friends?'

'Yes, we were. About the same age, of course, so we could talk about the war, hark back to memories the young find so boring to listen to.'

'Did she tell you about her husband?'

'No. Lulu was very cagey about personal matters and I hate to pry.'

'And Rory? He was a frequent visitor?'

'I wouldn't say *frequent*. He seemed to turn up unexpectedly. Lulu pretended to be cross with him, said he only came to borrow money, but she was fond of him, you could tell that. I saw Rory only four or five times. Once he knocked at my door to leave some birthday flowers for Lulu. She was out but Rory knew we were friends. It was nice for her to be thought of on her birthday, wasn't it? She had no one else.'

'He seemed genuinely fond of Mrs Starewska? Rich old widows sometimes attract the wrong types; con men, salesmen, you've heard the warning the police give out about trusting strangers, I'm sure.'

Mrs Sharpley looked aghast. 'Oh, Rory wasn't a stranger. Lulu told me she had known him since he was a student.'

'An attractive young man?'

She relaxed. 'No, you're quite wrong,

83

inspector. Rory was no toy boy. He's middle-aged, probably sixty, certainly retired or else he was unemployed. Lulu confided in me one evening after we'd had a little too much wine. She said she helped Rory out with jobs when he was hard up but he certainly didn't look hard up to me. A very smartly dressed gentleman, nicely spoken, but not smarmy, not at all. Oh no, inspector, Rory was no trickster only after Lulu's money. Did you find anything suspicious when you checked the flat?'

'Nothing so far. But it was extremely tidy. Was Mrs Starewska always so neat?'

The Sharpley smile hovered, her eyes lighting up with relish. 'Tidy? Lulu? Never! Unless Tizzy cleaned up twice a week the place would have sunk under the clutter. No, no. Poor Lulu had many qualities but housework was never her thing.'

'Tizzy's the cleaner?'

'Comes to us on Mondays and Thursdays but she wasn't here today for me, either. I expect she heard about the murder and took fright. A nervous little thing, hardly spoke an intelligible word. Armenian, I think. But a good worker and let Lulu's quick temper just roll off her like she never heard a word of it. Tizzy did for me and for a few other people on this floor, but I don't know where

Lulu found her. We paid Tizzy in cash each week and there was no contact number if either of us was away. I rather suspect we shan't see Tizzy here again.'

'She had no keys?'

'Heavens, no! Lulu warned me never to give access to anyone working in this building. She was a bit strange about it, seemed to think people were spying on her. She wouldn't even allow the caretaker to have a spare set but I believe she kept spare keys at the gallery for emergencies. I went along with Lulu's funny ways and I made sure I was always here when Tizzy was due and if Lulu was out I agreed to sit in her flat and watch Tizzy clean.'

'You had a key to number fifty-six yourself?'

'Until last month.'

'Why was that?'

'Lulu asked me to give the keys to Rory when he came to check her income tax returns.'

'He's an accountant?'

'I don't think so. She would have a proper accountant for the business, wouldn't she? No, I think Rory was trusted with things she didn't want her manager at the gallery to know about.'

Hayes rose to go and waited while Mrs

Sharpley opened the front door. 'Could you please phone me if Tizzy turns up again? I've a few questions. And one more thing. What is Rory's surname? We would like to ask him about his relationship with Mrs Starewska. I expect his telephone number is in her address book – my sergeant is going through her desk just now – but a full name would help.'

'I'm terribly sorry. I've never asked his surname and Lulu only gave me the telephone number of the gallery to call in an emergency.' She brightened. 'But I'm sure Rory will turn up soon – he was always popping in.'

Hayes hurried back to the Starewska flat and found the locksmith had been and gone.

'Two sets of keys but I kept the front entrance key separate, sir.' Bellamy handed over the new keys in a plastic envelope plus the original bunch now tagged with a label. 'Anything from the old girl next door?'

'Nothing much. What was in the desk?'

'Bank statements and some old tax returns. A passport and a wallet stuffed with Euros. Not enough for a spending spree and no other cash apart from two-fifty hidden in a box of tissues in the bathroom.'

'Two hundred quid! And that's all?'

Bellamy nodded. 'Petty cash?'

The doorbell rang. Two forensics officers introduced themselves and without more ado started dusting the flat for fingerprints. Hayes and Bellamy waited for them to finish, taking turns in the only armchair to watch the evening news, Hayes growing increasingly impatient as the time dragged by.

'There won't be anything here, Bellamy. Like I said, this bloke's too fly to leave dabs all over the place. Mrs Sharpley withdrew her complaint when Bass got so sharp but I believe her. I'm sure someone let himself in here on Sunday night and had a good look round. Only mistake was to leave the place too neat. Starewska was no housework freak and as the cleaner wasn't due until after the weekend I bet she drove off to the cottage and left it for the girl to clear up today.'

'What cleaner?'

'Some cash-in-hand character, probably an illegal Lulu found from somewhere. Anyway, the cleaner's scarpered. We might as well go home, Bellamy, these boys dabbing the furniture are never going to find any bloody fingerprints.'

But he was wrong. The senior officer called Hayes and indicated faint marks on the glass surface of the dressing table.

'Just a couple of handprints but clear enough, chief inspector. We'll fax the evidence to your base in Renham, OK? Copies to the local nick, of course. For Inspector Bass.'

Twelve

Superintendent Waller had taken it upon himself to set up a mobile incident facility opposite Starewska's cottage on the Green. Hayes was not pleased. Apart from the inconvenience of being away from his own office, he shared a pessimistic view of such blatant police presence with Sergeant Buller, a uniformed man nearing retirement, who had lived on the outskirts of Renham for the whole of his working life and was what the locals regarded 'a proper village bobby', the sort who thought nothing of spending half an hour a couple of times a week in the back room of The Mermaid, chewing the fat.

'No one's going to stroll into Waller's portacabin in full view of every nosy parker in the village,' Ted Buller bitterly remarked to Bellamy. 'Fucking waste of time, Roy, you see if I'm not right. Hayes'd be wiser to hang about the village shop, it's like bloody Coronation Street on pensions pay-out day.'

Roy Bellamy nodded, wondering if Chief Inspector Hayes was the right bloke for this sort of backwoods investigation at all. Oxford was, he privately concluded, more the DCI's scene; a city place ripe with city crime and city low-life. It had never come out why Hayes had been transferred from Oxford in the first place. Rumour was rife, but no insider information had leaked about any disciplinary action, and the last person to snatch a senior man like Hayes on to his own patch was Superintendent Waller. Chalk and cheese. Rough and too bloody smooth by half.

Hayes breezed in just after nine, frowning at the set-up in the mobile incident room, with its battery of computers, desks, and trestle tables jostling the limited space. As a working environment it suited no one, and the glum faces of his team reflected an investigation that seemed to be going no-where.

Preston had bagged a partitioned sector earmarked for the boss and, after a quick debriefing of the expectant murder squad assembled in the hope of a lead of some sort, Hayes stepped briskly into his temporary bolt-hole to review the situation. Preston followed him through with his notebook and itemized a suggested hit list starting with Renham CID's favourite redhead, Jenny Robbins.

'And I got this list for you, sir. The names of the local lads you asked for, the kids meeting in the bus shelter at weekends.'

'Right. Leave it with Bellamy, will you? He can round them up, see what they've got to say.' Hayes curtly nodded and turned his attention to the report on the fingerprint search of Starewska's flat.

Preston coughed and stood his ground. 'I took the liberty of having a word with a couple of them round the pool table at The Mermaid last night, sir. Kids my own boy knows from school. A difficult bunch, up to no good most of the time, I've warned our Tim to steer clear of them. One blighter was a bit more co-operative, though. A shifty little tyke called Darren Porter, lives with his mum up on the estate. Followed me outside and asked if there was any reward!'

Hayes laughed. 'Fat chance. Do you think he's got anything useful?'

Preston shrugged. 'Difficult to say. But he's the only one to look over the brick wall we've come up against on the house-to-house, sir. Anyway, Darren says he'll only talk to "Uncle Buller". Cheeky bugger.'

Hayes shrugged and gave the go-ahead. 'OK, put Buller on to it. Get him to shake down each of these bad lads individually, break up this gang culture posing. He's clearly the only uniform they're prepared to swap any information with.'

Preston left, shutting the door a bit too firmly, setting the flimsy partition wall awobble. Hayes cursed and started to unravel Bellamy's notes on their interview with Raoul Musset.

Jenny Robbins knocked at the door, her eyes sparking with irritation.

Hayes called to 'leave the bloody door, Robbins. No point in pretending every word spoken in here isn't as clear as a bell to the whole unit, not that there's any break-through to set the place alight. Trouble is the death of an octogenarian and her pet pussy cat is not remotely sexy, is it? A nice juicy murder of a prostitute strangled on the commissioner's doorstep would be more likely to set pulses racing.'

Jenny was clearly furious, her temper un-assuaged by Hayes' stab at black humour. It wasn't even funny. Old ladies no more de-served to be attacked than a skinny teenager gang-raped on her way home from a night out clubbing.

Hayes sobered. 'OK, what's your problem, Jenny?'

'It's Mrs Cox. She's cancelled our appointment to file her statement this morning. Says she's going to Heathrow to meet her husband and can't say when she'll be back, although I assume they'll have to be home for the weekend when her stepson gets back from his school trip.'

Hayes stifled an expletive and tried to calm things down. After a further fusillade, Robbins eventually cooled off and produced a faxed copy of the obituary and the grainy photographs borrowed from the professor. 'I promised to return the pictures to Mark Morrison, my press contact, this evening, sir.'

Hayes glanced at the obituary and shuffled the snapshots, returning them without a word. Jenny hurried round the desk and leant over his shoulder. 'This is our victim in the sixties with a party of university bods on some sort of symposium in Eastern Europe. The young bloke was her fancy boy, who tagged along for the ride. Possibly had a record, according to Professor Stenning. I think he mentioned his name was Smyth.'

'Didn't you take notes?'

'Hardly seemed relevant, sir, all that time ago. I'm sure a woman as good looking as our Lulu had a whole raft of admirers. The marriage didn't seem to last. I'm trying to track down information about her ex –

possibly the nearest to a next-of-kin – but it's difficult.'

'Did this chap Morrison have anything to help us?'

'I asked about Starewska's business methods but he knew very little, only snippets from Tessa Cox, who was a girlfriend of his before her marriage. They are still on good terms. He said Tessa let slip that Lulu personally collected any valuable items from her agent in Paris, a man called Dmitri, who is reluctant to come to the UK possibly because of visa problems in the past. There is another courier, name unknown, who helps out occasionally, but Tessa was never forthcoming about her dealing with Starewska and it's only since the murder that Mark Morrison has even thought about it.'

Hayes checked his watch and parcelled Robbins off to liaise with Bellamy on a computer search for anything they could dig up on Dmitri. When she had left he crossed to the window and gazed out at the flurries of snow drifting against the glass, and wondered if the fast-approaching Christmas break would reduce the investigation to a series of half-hearted forays into the miasma threatening to befog even the most prosaic of enquiries. Christmas was a bummer; witnesses scattered to family get-togethers, offices closed, normal lines of communication snagged by days, sometimes a whole week, of jollification. Even the Renham nick was already festooned with tinsel and balloons, though Waller had banned any mistletoe even at Buller's retirement party at the end of the month.

As if on cue, the man himself burst in, effectively blocking off Hayes' lair like a bung in a barrel, and dispelling, at a stroke, any notion that Hayes had even a temporary space to call his own. Waller claimed the chair behind the desk as Hayes spun round from his snow-gazing reveries.

'Right, Hayes. What have we got here?'

Hayes pulled up a chair and lit a cigarette, pulling his sparse résumé of the investigation around him like a comfort blanket.

'Ah, well, sir ... The old woman died from multiple stab wounds some time before, or just after, midnight on Saturday. Acid burns to the face indicate a degree of sadism difficult to square with the situation as nothing seems to have been stolen.'

'Sex, Hayes. Sex. That's at the bottom of all these random hits on women.'

'But she was over eighty years old!'

Waller rapped his temple in a knowing gesture. 'You don't get it, do you, Hayes? Gerontophilia,' he said, fixing his DCI in fierce focus. 'Someone who feels sexual attraction to old people; paedophiles in reverse. Instead of lusting after young girls these crackpots prey on old women.' Waller blew his nose in a trumpet of disgust. 'Unbelievable.'

Hayes looked away, wondering how to phrase it, Waller clearly utterly serious. He turned back.

'Yes, sir, absolutely right. But in this case the lady was not sexually assaulted, the autopsy was clear.'

Waller leant back expansively. 'The killer was rejected, she fought back as any poor woman would, and the attacker lost his temper and killed her.'

'There were no defensive wounds,' Hayes flatly put in. 'And how do we explain the acid?'

Waller became obdurate. 'A threat.'

'Y ... yes, that would fit. Actually, sir, I'm on my way to Oxford now; I'm expecting Mrs Starewska's manager to identify the body for us. I'm meeting him at the mortuary at eleven.' Parrying Waller's clear suspicion that he was taking yet more evasive action, Hayes waffled on about his visit to the gallery and Robbins' interview with the professor. Waller seemed unimpressed and skipped through the reports on the desk before irritably enquiring, 'No witnesses, Hayes? Not one person in this godforsaken village saw a single suspicious stranger hanging about?'

Hayes clutched at a straw. 'As a matter of fact we do have a likely sighting. One of the village lads has information but will only talk to Sergeant Buller. We're on to it now, sir. Buller's just the right man to winkle out the truth from any yobs hanging about the bus stop. You must excuse me now, sir. It's started to snow and, as you know, the traffic gets awfully snarled up the nearer we get to Christmas.'

Waller swallowed hard, determined to stay in control. 'This manager of hers, a sensible chap, is he? Not likely to throw a fit viewing a corpse?'

'The best we've got, sir. The friend who found the body, Mrs Cox, has gone to London to meet her husband at the airport, and we've been unable to trace any next-of-kin.' Hayes stood up and shuffled towards the door. 'Perhaps, as you're here, sir, you would like to debrief the team yourself? Something I might have missed?' he temptingly added.

Waller nodded sagely and instructed Hayes to send in Sergeant Preston on his way out. 'Keep me informed, Hayes, and that's an order. I don't want to find myself out on a limb with this case. The commissioner has already expressed anxiety about possible repercussions.'

On this dark note Hayes strode to his car, wondering what devious trick Waller had hatched with his buddy the commissioner, a man Hayes knew only too well was keen to bounce him right off the planet, into the arms of the Met, given half a chance.

Thirteen

Hayes was twenty minutes late for his appointment with Starewska's manager at the morgue.

'I am so sorry, Mr Musset. An unavoidable delay – I do apologize.'

Raoul Musset rose from his seat in the waiting room, casting aside a copy of *Reader's Digest* with admirable patience, his manner both pleasant and suitably reverent. He wore a dark suit and black tie, a gesture, Hayes concluded, that would be entirely lost on Lulu Starewska laid out on a mortuary trolley.

'Now, are you quite sure you are happy to do this, Mr Musset? In the absence of any next-of-kin the coroner may require a second identification, but your co-operation now is much appreciated.'

Musset raised his hand in wordless acquiescence and Hayes' mind momentarily alighted on the problem of securing a second witness to put a name to the corpse.

'If I may ask you to wait just a few more minutes while I make sure everything's ready?'

Hayes hurried into the side room set aside for such macabre viewings and collared a mortuary attendant. 'Hey, Colin, all set up for my witness? The old lady?'

The man nodded. 'We've done our best, chief, but she's not a pretty sight.'

'No matter. My chap seems reasonably composed.'

He retraced his steps and waited while Musset finished a couple of phone calls on his mobile. He led Musset through. Lulu had been laid out under a sheet that covered all but her head. The lighting focussed on the sad disarray of her wispy grey hair, so thin in fact that glimpses of the scalp were visible despite a bandage masking the worst of the pathologist's surgical intervention. Her face was almost unrecognizable, the ivory pallor resembling that of a marble effigy, the clotted burn scars blackening her neck and cheek.

Hayes gripped Musset's elbow as he stumbled, almost falling.

'My God,' he whispered. 'It's not possible! What happened to her face? I thought she had been stabbed – that's what it said on the news.'

'Shall we dispose of the formalities, sir, and then we can go to a private room and I can explain?'

Musset muttered an identification and Hayes led him out, nodding to the attendant to return his star turn to her refrigerated cabinet.

He ordered something hot and sweet for Musset and propelled him to an empty office. The man's colour was ashen, his breathing alarmingly rasping. A young woman brought in a tray of tea and Hayes passed a cup to Musset, who accepted with shaking fingers, the cup rattling on the saucer like chattering teeth. Hayes urged him to sugar it generously. 'It will calm your nerves, Mr Musset. I'm sorry to have to inflict such an experience on you.'

Raoul looked up, his eyes bloodshot, clearly shattered.

'I never expected my poor Madame to be so transformed. Such a cruel, cruel thing...'

Musset loosened his tie and sipped the tea, sweat glistening on his upper lip, but slowly regaining a little composure at last.

'You must explain to me what happened, chief inspector.'

Hayes paused and then laid as much information before his witness as seemed unavoidable. 'Well, first of all, I must impress upon you that enquiries are still in progress and consequently any facts I share with you are strictly confidential. We are anxious to keep the details of the murder out of the public domain at present.'

'I understand.'

'The official line is unequivocal. The lady died from multiple stab wounds. The alarming possibility remains that she was tortured beforehand. A quantity of corrosive acid was flicked onto her face as she was held down.'

'Oh my God! What sort of monster would do such a thing to a defenceless old woman?'

'It's early days, Mr Musset, and the killer will, I assure you, be caught. At present we have to assume that the assailant was threatening Mrs Starewska with the acid in order to discover hidden cash. We have been assured that the lady kept no valuables either at her London flat or at the cottage, but it is impossible to know what, if anything, was taken. You did mention that Mrs Starewska arrived in England as a penniless refugee. With such a background would she be in the habit of keeping money – or even portable items such as diamonds – hidden on the premises?'

Musset shook his head. 'I have no idea but

I rather doubt it. Perhaps she had a safety deposit box at the bank or abroad and the burglar was desperate to have access to it?'

Hayes doubted this but pressed Musset for more background information.

'There is a strong possibility that her flat was burgled during the weekend but there again we have no proof of anything missing. Could you direct me to her agent? A man called Dmitri, I believe, who operated from Paris.'

'Dmitri was Madame's business. The acquisition of artworks was a secret operation she kept to herself. My role was that of a salesperson. To strengthen contacts within the trade and to flatter our regular clients.'

'Who were?'

'Mostly Eastern Europeans either living in London or having business interests here. The gallery was unique. If a wealthy collector wanted a certain type of decoration he inevitably came to us. Madame left that side of things to me; her flair was outsourcing interesting items, arranging for them to be upgraded for sale and dictating a wide profit margin. Her expenses were extensive as our accountants will confirm, but frankly, dear sir, my role was almost that of a sleeping partner. Madame invited no curiosity about her means of purchase and I knew better than to overstep the mark. I never met Dmitri.'

Hayes sighed. 'How about an Englishman called Rory?'

He shook his head. 'Sounds like one of Madame's TV contacts, the young men who invited her to appear on discussion programmes? Sorry, inspector, the name means nothing to me.'

'OK. Now, does Professor Stenning ring a bell?'

'Ah yes. A prestigious art historian who sometimes authenticated paintings for us.'

'Smyth?'

Musset shrugged. 'Sorry. As I say, Madame kept her contacts to herself. Have you checked her address book?'

Hayes decided that his sitting duck was getting much too comfortable and tossed a pebble into the water. 'Now, I have to ask you, Mr Musset, for a sworn statement regarding your movements last weekend. Also, for elimination purposes, your fingerprints.' He targeted the unfortunate man with a final throw. 'You do realize, of course, that the likeliest motive for Mrs Starewska's attack was to extract information regarding your very profitable business, and as the sole beneficiary I feel it is my duty to warn you to secure yourself as best you can.

Additional alarms at the gallery? Extra precautions at home? An acid attack is a rare form of threat in this country and I would be abusing your trust if I pretended that an assailant such as we have here is not sufficiently vicious to pursue his quest to your door. Are you quite certain, sir, that you are not withholding any information regarding Mrs Starewska's business methods?'

Musset had visibly paled, his temporary aplomb now in total disarray in the face of Hayes' deliberate scare tactics. 'You think he may come after me next?'

Hayes rose and opened the door. 'I am, I must admit, a novice in understanding the line of business that would attract such criminals, but the fact remains your employer was tortured and killed. Nothing was stolen either from the cottage or from her flat. That only leaves the gallery. I suggest you be on your guard, Mr Musset, and double your precautions.'

He ushered the man out with a final blow. 'My sergeant, DS Bellamy, will take your statement together with your fingerprints at the station. May I offer you a lift or can you find your own way to Renham? I assume you drove here?'

Musset nodded, his parting glance one of

confusion aggravated by Hayes' firm, albeit sympathetic, handshake.

Hayes wandered along the corridor to seek out the pathologist, Doctor Johnson. The door of the lab was open, his quarry leaning over a bench on which partly burnt clothing was pinned out on a sheet. He looked up, removing his bifocals with a flourish, his warm smile the first cheerful greeting Hayes had met with all day.

'Hey, Roger. Nasty mess this old lady murder, eh? Any leads?'

'Not much. I'm reduced to putting the fear of God into one of my witnesses. The case is bound up in a line of business I barely comprehend and everyone involved is worried some dirty dealings will tumble out of the woodwork. Any luck with the acid?'

Oliver Johnson grinned, his enthusiasm a miracle to Hayes in view of the work the medic faced each day; delving into decomposing guts, examining the fluff and threads of fabric that might well prove the turning point in any forensic investigation.

'Actually, old son, I've had a call from the vet.'

Hayes grimaced. 'Don't tell me. He's done an autopsy on the bloody cat.'

'The cat's not dead.'

'Really? Another eight lives to go, then. Fancy that. It had all but croaked last time I saw it.'

'A neighbour took it to the vet in Renham and he patched it up. Sent me a sample of the matted fur and I got my bloke to analyse the acid.'

'Battery fluid?'

'Nothing so ordinary, Roger. The stuff thrown over our corpse was a specially virulent type used by painters and decorators to strip varnish. Your killer's a bloody house painter, or someone in the trade; the stuff's too strong for general sale. He's sending me a list of possible suppliers as soon as he can track them down. Any good to you?'

Hayes all but whooped with joy, throwing a playful punch to Johnson's shoulder with an over-enthusiastic fist.

'OK, OK, Roger. Don't get too excited, chances are there will be hundreds of outlets distributing this stuff – and not necessarily all British either. It's not exactly going to pinpoint this sadistic beggar. Bear in mind, the acid on the cat was deliberate. The vet identified injuries indicating the poor beast was held down and in its fright all but strangled itself trying to escape.'

'Do you think the cat was tortured in front of the old woman? A prompt to get her to give up whatever he was after?'

Johnson hedged his bets. 'It's been known but I can at least confirm that the acid was inflicted *before* the stabbing and, if a threat was the motive, shooting corrosive at the eyes of your victim is a pretty powerful incentive to spill the beans, wouldn't you say?'

Hayes drew back. 'Any more good news, Oliver?'

'I think we've got a good idea of the type of knife used. Evidence of the rivets show up under magnification. I've faxed some interesting photographs to you and a possible description of the sort of weapon you're looking for.'

Fourteen

Later that evening Sergeant Buller picked up Darren Porter at a disused petrol station outside Renham. The boy wore a football supporters' shirt under an oil-stained denim jacket, his spiky peroxided hair shining like a halo under the street lights.

'Hop in, lad, it's brass monkeys out there. You look like a frozen fillet just off the slab. Ride here on your bike, did you?' He fished under the dashboard and brought out a bag of hot chips. 'Here, finish these off – you could do with feeding up by the look of you.'

Darren *did* look a poor specimen, a scrawny youth, small for his age. He got in the car and tucked into the chips with gusto, nervously glancing round the empty fore-court as Buller accelerated away.

They pulled into a lay-by a couple of miles down the road and Darren tossed the greasy wad of chip paper out of the window and fished in his pocket for a packet of Marlboro. He lit up, eyeing Buller with insolence. 'How much of a sweetener do I get for helping you out like this, Mr Buller?'

'Depends. Just spit it out, Darren, and then we'll decide. I haven't got all bloody night so make it quick.'

The lad sucked on his cigarette, his fingernails bitten to the quick, the rank smell of his trainers ripening in the overheated interior of Buller's Fiesta. Buller was in mufti, all bundled up in a sheepskin coat, a tweed cap pulled down low over his eyes. He had known the Porter kids since they'd first featured on his complaints list, real tearaways, but who was to blame? Four boys left for their mum to drag up as best she could, Billy Porter long gone. Darren, the youngest and the runt of the litter, was left to his own devices after finally being chucked out of school after years of truancy and bouts of shoplifting that Buller had, over time, done his best to smooth over with the magistrate, his sympathy with Rosie Porter at odds with the superintendent's demands for a crackdown.

The cigarette fumes were getting to him and he rolled down the window despite the cold. 'Come on, lad, stub out that fag, I'm trying to give up.'

Darren threw the burning stub out to join

the chip wrapper in the gutter, and finally got stuck into his story.

'Well, it was like this, Mr Buller. Last Saturday I got the sack, see, from my job at Frewins. "Don't need you no more, Darren," that old fucker Frewin said. No warning. Nuffin'. Just "Sling your 'ook, mate. And I've docked your wages to even up on the fags you've pinched." Sodding lies, Mr Buller. Anyhow, I was skint after my mum had shaken me down and I couldn't go to The Mermaid with nuffin' in my pocket, could I? I watched a video in the back room but my mum wouldn't have me hanging round with that new boyfriend of hers knocking at the door so I decided to push off and have a bit of fun on my own. I crossed the Green and jogged off down the lane to the river.'

'The footpath that runs behind the old woman's cottage? What you doing down there – poaching?'

Darren giggled. 'Me? What gives you that idea, Sarg? No, a bit of wildlife.'

'Meeting Pauline Denner in the woods, Darren? How d'you swing that? I thought she had given you the push?'

'Nah, nature watching.'

'In the dark? What time was this nature watching of yours?'

'Must've been about half past twelve. I'd pinched a Cornish pasty and a beer on my way out – Mum owed me that, Mr Buller, shoving me out with no money and nuffin' to eat, she owed me – and I settled down to watch.'

'Watch what?'

'Foxes. Badgers if I was lucky. They come out at night, see, scuffle about down by the river, a whole bloody circus down there if you're quiet. I 'ad my torch but I daresn't show a light and you have to keep as quiet as a dead'un or the buggers are off in a flash.'

'Not badger baiting, are you, Darren? Nasty game that, get you into no end of trouble.'

'Not me, Mr Buller. I love animals. No, it was my secret, see. I don't let on to the others, they'd be down there with their shovels and dogs quick as lightning. No, I just watch 'em and if there's a full moon like Saturday night, you don't need no torch anyway. And I had my grandad's binoculars he give me when he couldn't go to the races no more. Freezing it was, but better'n hangin' about down at the bus stop in case the boys decided to have a bit of a booze-up after the pub turned out.'

'Too cold, eh? Pity that. If you and the lads

had been partying on the Green last Saturday you might have seen something worth me shelling out for.'

Darren squeezed Buller's arm, cunning as a ferret. 'Don't you worry, Mr Buller, it's your lucky day.' He started to nibble his thumbnail, frowning out into the darkness, savouring Buller's rapt attention. 'I settled myself down behind some brambles and stuff – there's not much cover this time of year and them badgers are so sharp they scoot off back down their hole if you so much as break a twig. Anyhow, like I said, there was a bright moon, shining on the river, it was, making everything all silver. I didn't see the boat at first, it was tied up to a willow and hidden under branches hanging over the water, nobody aboard. So I crept down the bank to have a butchers. Nice smart boat an'all, all white paint and with the name clear as daylight. *Stargazer*. Never seen a boat like that round this way and I was thinkin' to myself I'd just climb aboard and see what it was like inside.'

Buller raised an eyebrow but kept quiet, letting Darren spin it out.

'But then I hear this bloke come crashing through the trees like a bloody bull in a china shop and I scramble up the bank and crouch in the bushes.

'I sat as still as I could, hardly breaking wind, Mr Buller, pissing myself in case it was the gamekeeper from the big house doing a late run to catch them gypos they reckon've been night fishing. I thought to myself, there goes your chance of seeing badgers, Darren. I watched this bloke untie the motor boat, wondering what he was up to, taking my eye off the ball, Mr Buller, which was a big mistake because, next I knew, someone had me round the throat, grabbed me from behind and shoved me arse over tit into the brambles. Couldn't shout nor nothin' and with all the commotion the geezer on the boat jumped off and run over to see what was up.'

'Did you recognize him?'

'No local for sure, Mr Buller. A great big bugger in a fur hat he was, lit up by a torch the pig who had 'old of me was trying to shine in my face. I was fighting like crazy and managed to half rip off one sleeve of his top, which made him really mad, but he wouldn't let go and for a minute I thought he'd bloody strangle me. Then the guy in the Davy Crockett 'at called him off and the pig threw me a rabbit punch, which fair winded me, and I fell on the floor and he put the boot in. I lay there, winded like I said, but kept my 'ead down till I heard the boat roar off up river. But I got a bloody good look at one of the pig's arms when he was holding me down. Tattooed from wrist to elbow, which was as far as I could see, but I bet he was done all over like that bloke in *The Guinness Book of Records*.'

'Did the big man shout out a name when he called the other one off you?'

Darren shook his head, his eyes fixing on Buller with dismay at the recollection of what, Buller guessed, had scared him shitless despite the cocky stance.

'Would you recognize them? Could you pick out the men in an ID parade?'

'Blimey, Mr Buller, I don't have to make it official, do I? My mates'd kill me if they found out I was a fuckin' snout. I thought you could just pay me for a quiet bit of info, no questions asked. These blokes were not from round 'ere, chances are they're miles away by now.'

'But you saw the fur hat man clear enough in the moonlight, didn't you? You're a bit of an artist, Darren, I've seen those cartoons you've done for your pals, you've a real gift, boy. How about doing a sketch for me, just a bit of a picture, something for me to show the boss? Here,' he said, scrabbling under the dashboard for something to write on. He grabbed a bus timetable and folded it

115

back to a page of adverts. 'Look, on this blank bit, Darren, just see what's still clear in your mind. Start with the hat and the rest'll come back to you, you see if it don't.'

He passed over a biro and Darren reluctantly poised it above the wide expanse of sky pictured above a photograph of their local stately home, Bartram Court.

Buller dropped his dubious informant back at the deserted garage to pick up his bike. Twenty quid seemed a fair whack for the only eye-witness account to surface so far, even if the strangers with the motor boat turned out to be no more dangerous than another pair of bloody poachers. Darren perked up after the pay-off and, as a bonus, Buller promised to get him another job.

'You as good at washing cars as joyriding, Darren? I've got a mate at Renham Motors who owes me a favour. He'd be glad of a good worker but on my say-so he'd expect the best. I'll ring him in the morning and say you'll be at the garage at ten sharp, OK? Don't let me down, Darren, it might be the last chance you'll get, and if you play your cards right Mr Dudley'll give you a chance in the workshop. How about that, then? You tell your mum Sergeant Buller's putting in a good word for you, eh?'

Unlike Buller's efforts, Jenny Robbins' date with Mark Morrison that evening turned out to be of absolutely no use in progressing the investigation. They met at a bistro in Thame and Jenny dutifully returned the professor's photographs, carefully omitting any reference to the murder. In fact, Mark Morrison was far from curious about the case and quickly suggested they caught the last showing of a Woody Allen movie at a film club in Oxford.

'I've been a member since I worked there for a year, a research project at the Ashmolean. No money in it, but good for my CV and there's always plenty of cheap entertainments to latch on to if you know the ropes. Private views are the best freebies; champagne and enough canapés to pass for supper if you're lucky.'

Jenny gradually warmed to Morrison and after a post-cinema curry and a nightcap at his very upmarket, all expenses paid, hotel, she drove home with a warm glow equalling Ted Buller's assessment of an evening by no means wasted.

Fifteen

Hayes assembled his murder squad for a run-down of progress so far. Ted Buller's possible eye witness was the only lead likely to bring any satisfaction and the entire team was directed to pursue a search throughout a twenty-mile radius for any hire companies to have rented out a motor vessel over the weekend. December was hardly boating weather and even private craft were mostly laid up for the winter, so sightings of a motor launch cruising the river at night would be thin on the ground. Even so, it was a long shot, and Darren's sketch of his furry-hatted assailant was hardly an identi-kit picture.

Superintendent Waller was like a cat on hot bricks, all too aware that unless the killer was caught before Christmas the trail would inevitably grow cold, even the initial media interest in an old woman's horrific murder buried under yuletide cheer. It look-ed like stalemate; no motive, no theft and no background history to back up Hayes' hunches about the dubious international trade conducted from the Star Gallery. Tessa Cox and her husband had gone to ground with no forwarding address and only Jenny Robbins' assurance that their boy was due back from his school trip at the weekend offered any hope of their return. Questions remained unanswered from that quarter and Starewska's private life seemed to have been deliberately shrouded in mystery.

Hayes decided to keep up the pressure on Raoul Musset and phoned the gallery several times without success. On Friday morning he was informed that the line was unobtainable, which put his temper into overdrive. What was the slimy bugger playing at? He retrieved the keys to Starewska's flat from the filing cabinet where Bellamy had placed them, together with the business card of Musset's lawyer, and picked up the phone again.

'Good morning. Mr Ball? This is Chief Inspector Hayes, Thames Valley Police. Your client, Mr Musset, entrusted me with some keys and I wondered if you could let me have his mobile phone number? I've been trying to reach him at the gallery but I believe he intended to close for business until after Mrs Starewska's funeral.'

The pause was like the hush between lightning and a thunder clap and the subdued tones of Ball's reply were almost inaudible.

Hayes attempted to reconnect. 'Pardon me, Mr Ball, I didn't quite catch that. Could you speak up, please? We seem to have a bad line.'

'I said, Haven't you people got your act together? I thought the police was co-ordinating enquiries these days.'

Hayes choked back a stiff rejoinder, wondering if the usual armed truce between lawyers and the police had been superseded by some new EU directive.

'Sorry?'

'Surely, Chief Inspector whatever-your-name-is, you must accept *some* responsibility for the suicide. Your treatment of the poor man reduced him to abject terror.'

'Just tell me what's happened, Mr Ball. I've just got in this morning and I have a complicated murder to investigate. Has Mr Musset had an accident?'

'I think you should come here straight away, chief inspector. The local investigating officer wishes to speak with me and I've agreed to a meeting at the gallery at noon. I suggest you be there to explain your part in all this. There are aspects of this dreadful situation on which only you can throw any light.'

The solicitor's voice grew querulous and Hayes guessed his unseen accuser to be an older man, a man unused to the dramatic events that the Starewska death had precipitated into the quiet backwater of a lawyer's office.

'I admit I bear some responsibility myself, inspector,' he continued. 'Through no fault of my own I had disappointing news to impart and perhaps I could have phrased it more diplomatically, but Mr Musset was in a highly agitated state when he arrived in my office yesterday and my advice was the final blow.'

'Forgive me, Mr Ball, but the situation is still unclear. Are you telling me Mr Musset is dead?'

'Suicide. He killed himself at the gallery. Set fire to the premises and perished.'

'I'll come straight away!'

Hayes slammed down the receiver and told Bellamy to fetch the car. 'We're going to the gallery. Leave a message with Preston, I don't want to have to explain anything to Waller before I've got the full story.'

They arrived at the gallery with half an hour

to spare, and Hayes, dogged by Bellamy, pushed past the police cordon to seek the man in charge. A fire engine blocked the road, hoses snaking into the building, the door standing open and a scene of devastation on view to a number of curious bystanders. The fire had been extinguished but the soot-blackened interior had been all but gutted, a charred stair carpet presumably leading to further destruction on the upper floor.

A stern-faced police officer barred his way. Hayes produced his ID card.

'Chief Inspector Hayes. Mr Musset's solicitor arranged to meet me here at twelve. Are you in charge here?'

After a terse exchange the sergeant called upstairs. 'Sir. There's an officer from Thames Valley here to see you. Says he's expected.'

A plain clothes officer appeared at the head of the stairs and beckoned Hayes to join him and another man later introduced as the fire investigation officer. Bellamy was instructed to wait outside for Mr Ball.

The upper floor was in ruins but still bore the remnants of a bed-sitting room, the smoke-stained walls and squelching carpet underfoot the result of a disaster aggravated by the efforts of the fire department to quell it. The stench of scorched fabric hung in the air despite the broken windows, splintered by the heat, which allowed a freezing blast of air to cause Hayes to button his coat.

The three men stood silently in the centre of the room, gazing round at the devastation. They introduced themselves to each other.

'Inspector Mayhew,' Hayes said, 'I'm not sure I have all the facts here. Mr Ball, the solicitor, seemed to think I could help. Could you explain what happened?'

The fire investigation officer jumped the gun, eager to put his version of events, and led Hayes to the door of a small washroom. 'The victim started the fire downstairs, leaving the front door unlocked for a quick getaway. But the blaze got out of hand and he fled up here, locking himself in the washroom.'

'Arson?' Hayes snapped. 'I was told it was suicide.'

The fire investigation officer stiffened, suddenly on the defensive. 'I have a great deal of experience in this area, chief inspector, and the evidence is clear. An accelerant was splashed around the showroom and inexpertly fired. Arson, no question. Started downstairs soon after midnight, the alarm being raised by a neighbour, but it quickly got out of control despite the fire department's swift response. The perpetrator had no idea how quickly a fire takes hold, clearly a man with no experience of fire raising, certainly not one of our regular arsonists such as a professional hired to facilitate an insurance claim, nor local tearaways in it either for a buzz or holding a malicious grudge against the shop owner.'

'But Mr Musset would not normally be on the premises at night, would he, so it was unlikely to have been a personal vendetta?' Hayes put in. 'He had a home to go to and a fancy antique shop would hardly attract the venom of yobs, surely?'

Mayhew butted in. 'Hang on there, chief inspector. Do you have a view on this? I understand our victim drove to Oxford recently to identify the body of the owner of this gallery and, according to Mr Ball, was in a very nervous frame of mind when he called at the solicitor's office yesterday. Mr Ball says his client was officially warned to upgrade the security here. Did you have reason to frighten the man? A tip-off?'

Hayes shrugged. 'Nothing specific. The sight of his employer's body was enough to upset anyone and I thought it my duty while the killer is still at large to advise Mr Musset to watch his back. But arson? Why would he do that? Mr Musset benefited from the death of Mrs Starewska, his ownership of the gallery was assured.'

The fire officer began to protest, insisting that his opinion was substantiated. At that moment the constable on the main door called up to Mayhew.

'Mr Ball's here, sir.'

'Ask him to go through to the office downstairs.' Mayhew turned to the fire officer. 'You have finished up here, haven't you? You're satisfied to file your report and pass the final enquiries to us?'

The fire officer nodded, leading the way down the damaged stairway and rejoining his team, who lounged around the fire engine waiting for orders.

Hayes shook hands with Mr Ball and confirmed his hunch. Ball *was* an old guy, grey haired and visibly trembling with shock as he was led through the ruined showroom to the back office, which remained remarkably untouched. Inspector Mayhew ushered them inside and closed the door, pulling up a seat for the older man, who placed a briefcase at his feet and subsided on one of Musset's fragile gilt chairs with a sigh. Hayes stood by the door, allowing Mayhew to conduct the interview from behind the desk.

'May I start with my condolences, Mr

Ball? This has been a nasty shock for you. Was Mr Musset a long-standing client?'

'Actually, it was Mrs Starewska who retained my services. I occasionally bumped into Raoul at private views here. She was a generous lady and liked to host parties for valued customers to which I was sometimes invited.'

'Can you describe the clientele?'

'Oh, the usual types: foreign buyers, other dealers, media people, not the sort I normally meet in the course of my business, but Lulu liked to show off and knew I was fascinated by the strange world she inhabited. Lulu was an old friend and I thought I knew her.' He paused, gripping his knees.

'But her methods were cruel. She had promised poor Musset that he would inherit everything after she passed away. He slaved for more than fifteen years in expectation of ultimate reward, and I assumed she had warned him of the new will made two years ago. It was my sad duty to disabuse Raoul on Thursday of this week. As I told you, Inspector Mayhew, the poor man was already in a very anxious state following the warning from the chief inspector here, and the news I was forced to impart was such a severe shock he suffered an asthmatic attack in my office. I offered to call a doctor but after ten minutes or so he recovered sufficiently for me to call a taxi for him and that,' he said with finality, 'was the last I saw of the unfortunate soul. After years of hope he was tossed aside for an alleged next-of-kin. He said he would go back to Lebanon, try to start again, but clearly the financial cost was too great. Suicide was the only way out.'

Inspector Mayhew half rose then thought better of it, subsiding into Musset's throne-like chair and throwing a helpless glance at Hayes before making an attempt to alleviate the older man's distress.

'It was not suicide, Mr Ball. Mr Musset's death was an accident. He shut himself in the washroom to escape the fire but was overcome by fumes, aggravated no doubt by his asthma. He had abandoned a document case in here that contained private papers from his desk, his car keys and his passport. He must have been clearing out his belongings and a one-way ticket to Beirut would indicate that, far from suicide, Mr Musset had every intention of making a fresh start abroad.'

The solicitor looked up, his conscience allayed by this garbled account of Musset's death. Hayes wondered how the poor old guy would face up to the coroner's verdict. Arson was a dirty word and a wicked revenge on the person who had snatched away what Musset had thought to have been his inheritance.

Mr Ball rose unsteadily and, clasping the briefcase to his chest, prepared to leave. Hayes touched his arm, blocking his exit.

'Just one more thing, sir. You mention a will in favour of a person allegedly Mrs Starewska's next-of-kin. What is her name?'

'Oh, not a lady, chief inspector. Robert Smyth. He claims to be Lulu's son. Rory, she called him.'

Sixteen

After the solicitor had left, Hayes sent Bellamy off to get lattes from the local coffee-shop and settled down with Inspector Mayhew to tidy up the loose ends.

Mayhew lit a cigarette and settled behind Musset's desk. 'You seemed stunned by the old lady's change of heart. Leaving everything to her son sounds pretty fair to me. Did the name Smyth ring a bell?'

'A real clanger. The thing is this son of hers, if it's true, has been kept well out of the picture. Nobody, not even her oldest friend who wrote the obituary, twigged it. It's a bonus for me. With Musset dead I can call on this Robert Smyth to identify Mrs Starewska's body, which should satisfy the coroner. Trouble is there's a possibility this bloke's got form, my DC got a whiff of it from gossip about some old photographs, so if he claims to be the next-of-kin I shall need proof of identity. I don't suppose old man Ball checked it out, do you? Mrs Starewska was entitled to leave her money to any Tom, Dick or Harry. The solicitor wouldn't care whether Smyth was related or not.'

'He was very cut up about Raoul Musset. Convinced it was suicide. Do you go along with it, chief inspector?'

'Just call me Hayes, everyone does.' He gazed around the room, which was hardly damaged at all, merely harbouring a lingering tang of smoke like the bitter afterglow of spent fireworks. 'I'm not sure. Setting fire to the place would be understandable from Musset's point of view, I suppose. Starewska was, I gather, a difficult woman and Musset put up with being her dogsbody for years on the understanding that, if he kept his nose clean, everything would eventually be his. Not a sniff of anyone else likely to steal a march on him, let alone a long-lost son.'

'I suppose she lost touch and the prodigal turned up just in time to scoop the pool.'

'No. Smyth's been hanging round since the sixties at least, we've seen a picture of him as a student joining one of Starewska's research trips to the Balkans.'

Bellamy knocked at the door and trooped in with three lidded polystyrene beakers and placed them on the desk.

'Thanks, chum. Pull up a chair. The inspector and I were just comparing notes.

The fire investigating officer insists Musset accidentally topped himself after torching the gallery but I'm not convinced.'

Mayhew shifted nervously in his seat, feeling outnumbered, hoping this provincial detective wasn't going to pull rank and complicate everything. 'Why not?' he snapped.

Hayes sipped his coffee and quizzically eyed his reluctant co-investigator. 'First off, let's have a dekko at Musset's personal stuff, shall we? He was clearing out his desk, the fire officer seems to think, but when the smoke started to penetrate this back room Musset took fright and scarpered upstairs, which was a stupid thing to do; any fool knows a staircase acts like a chimney funnelling a fire, and Musset was well aware that the upstairs windows were barred so no escape there. An asthmatic would be the last person to kill himself deliberately by suffocating fumes, choking to death being his biggest nightmare, so we can rule out suicide straight away. Which leaves arson. So why was Musset wasting time clearing out his desk at this late stage? If he planned to fire-bomb the gallery he would have brought the petrol with him, wouldn't he? And even a man obsessed with ruining Smyth's inheritance would have the nous to clear out his stuff beforehand. What was so important that he was still saving papers from his desk when the place was likely to explode into flames?'

Mayhew pulled out a document case from a filing tray piled with evidence he needed to take back to the station, and emptied the contents on to the desk.

'See here, Hayes. Like I said, keys, some sales receipts, an address book and correspondence from the accountant. Nothing personal except his passport and an air ticket for a flight on Sunday.'

'Quite. But no mobile phone. He was glued to his phone, even took a couple of calls at the mortuary when I was with him. Not the type to be parted from his bloody phone, and if he was so frightened that he bolted upstairs he could have phoned for help.'

'Didn't want to be caught at the scene of an arson attack. Panicked. From Mr Ball's description of the poor bloke he was in a right old state all week. You met him, Hayes. Did he strike you as the sort to destroy the place from sheer malice?'

'Frankly no. He loved all the old tat they sold here. And I'll tell you something else that's missing apart from his mobile. Valuable stuff.'

Mayhew choked on his coffee. 'Eh?'

132

'You checked his car? Nothing interesting wrapped up in the boot?'

'Nothing. We had the car to pieces this morning. We also checked his flat. We were looking for a suicide note,' he grimly added.

'Well, last time I was here Musset pointed out two priceless icons that were hanging on the wall over there. Too rare to go on display, he said. They've gone. Not burnt to a crisp, the fire didn't reach here. Gone.'

'You think he cleared the pickings before setting fire to the place, assuming the loss would be lumped in with the rest of the damage? With his boss dead, Musset was probably the only person to have any sort of stock list.'

'It's a possibility. But unless your lot found the icons at his flat, they've gone. He could hardly smuggle them out of the country to Lebanon without questions being asked. Proof of ownership? An exit permit? There wasn't time for him to sell them on between hearing the bad news from Ball and deciding to pull out. The market for this sort of stuff is limited, unique artworks would be difficult to place at the drop of a hat, and with all the publicity about Starewska's murder followed up by any arson attempt Musset was planning as a means of masking any losses, a buyer would demand provenance at the very least.'

'What are you getting at, Hayes?'

'Well, if you don't find these pieces, chances are Musset wasn't here alone. But if he was alone why lock himself in the washroom?'

Mayhew stubbed out his cigarette and glared. 'Are you going to contest the fire inspector's report?'

Hayes shrugged and rose to go, smiling in that provocative way Bellamy recognized all too well. 'To be honest, mate, I've got enough on my plate already. I leave it with you, it's your case, whatever you decide suits me.'

Bellamy opened the door and Mayhew escorted them off the premises.

Back in the car Bellamy grinned and started the engine. Hayes was a cunning sod and no mistake. Throws a couple of spanners in the inspector's nice tidy arson case and leaves the poor bloke to pick up the pieces. 'Where to next, guv'?'

'Let's see if we can flush out this guy Smyth. First stop Mrs Sharpley at Starewska's block of flats and if she doesn't know where to find him we shall have to shake down that poor bloody solicitor.'

They parked on the square and walked

over to Starewska's apartment building. The day had brightened, a crisp breeze sending pale clouds scudding across the winter sky like feathers.

The doorman stood inside, his solid presence blanking the view of the dim foyer. He opened the door, regarding Hayes and Bellamy with suspicion. Hayes producing his card and presenting himself as a visitor for Mrs Sharpley did the trick, and the doorman called the lift for them himself, touching his peak cap with due deference.

'I'll ring through and tell Mrs Sharpley you're on your way up, sir.'

The lift doors clanged shut and the lift began its jolting progress to the first floor.

'Someone's put the wind up the management, Bellamy. Tightened security since last time we were here.'

'Perhaps Mr Smyth's been stamping round, checking up on his inheritance, sir.'

Hayes grinned and knocked at Mrs Sharpley's door, which was opened on the instant by a tall, heavily built man with the speed of a demon king popping up from a stage trapdoor.

Hayes held out his hand. 'Rory, I presume. What a coincidence. My sergeant was just talking about you.'

Seventeen

Mrs Sharpley hovered in the background, smiling, glad of all the unexpected company, Bellamy guessed. Hayes stood rooted to the doorstep, giving Smyth a quick once-over as introductions were effected all round.

'Won't you come in, chief inspector?' Rory invited. 'Mrs Sharpley has kindly made some tea.'

'I thought we should go next door for a quiet chat, if you don't mind. Mr Ball has explained your circumstances, Mr Smyth, but we shall need full details for the coroner.'

Rory smiled. 'Sorry, folks, but my keys don't fit. I can't let you in. But we can adjourn to a restaurant if you wish. Lunch, perhaps?'

Robert Smyth was a smooth operator with, Hayes sensed, years of experience of sliding out of difficult situations. Fraud, wasn't it? Got three years, according to Robbins' professor and, in Hayes' experience, the career of a con man was never quite extinguished after a spell in an open prison.

'I have keys to number fifty-six. We thought it necessary to change the locks after Mrs Sharpley's complaint regarding an intruder.'

Rory smiled, a nice warm grin. Good teeth, a bit of a yellowish winter tan, the sort of tan you get jetting around ski resorts. He nodded, excused himself to his elderly hostess and, reclaiming a camel-haired overcoat and a briefcase from Mrs Sharpley's hall chair, followed Hayes and Bellamy to Starewska's flat.

Bellamy opened up, returned the shiny new keys to his back pocket and stood aside to allow Hayes and Smyth to lead the way. The apartment was stuffy, the air spent like the flat atmosphere of a storeroom. But it was warm and Bellamy scratched around to find extra chairs so all three could settle in the lounge. Smyth claimed the armchair.

'Is my information correct in that you are Ludmilla Starewska's natural heir, Mr Smyth?'

'Absolutely.'

'And that your connection has, until now, been something of a secret? The late Mrs Starewska's friends seem to have been unaware of your existence.'

Rory smiled, easing back in the armchair and crossing his legs, entirely at ease and not a little amused by Hayes' stiff manner. 'My mother was an extremely private person, chief inspector, a born conspirator, I suspect. It added to the air of mystery she fostered. An enchanting attribute, though not everyone appreciated her lack of candour. My birth was her only mistake she was cruelly to admit to me once her cover was blown. I tracked her down, you see, not difficult as it happens and a driving compulsion for a young man that Lulu was not comfortable with at the start of our renewed acquaintanceship. But I persuaded her to make the best of it and, over the years, as long as I played the game and kept my embarrassing relationship between ourselves, my mother came to rely on me and, as I like to think, even to love me at the end.'

'She changed her will in your favour?'

'Only recently. She dangled the possibility before my eyes for years like a bright shining bauble just out of reach. But eventually I was given my due and, on the understanding that my future "expectations" remained a secret between us, the last few years have proved something of a family comedy, a joke Lulu wickedly savoured in the sleepless small hours of the night, she once admitted in a sentimental moment.'

'You were adopted at birth?'

Rory nodded. 'A private arrangement with childless friends who promised to provide the sort of stable background she herself had never enjoyed. Lulu was not the motherly type, chief inspector, but who am I to blame her? The Smyths were good people, I enjoyed an expensive education and, if my congenital weakness had not confounded all that solid English nurturing, I would never have lost my way, as my probation officer used to complain. Finding Lulu became an obsession and, after rifling through my parents' private papers, tracking down Ludmilla Starewska, which was her maiden name as it happens, was no problem at all.'

'She welcomed your appearance on the scene?'

'Not at first – the embarrassment of an illegitimate son on one's doorstep is hardly welcome. I was at Oxford at the time, in the process of flunking my final exams. I refused to go away and after a number of painful confrontations we came to an arrangement. Blood will tell, as the geneticists remind us. The only thing Lulu held out about was my father's identity. Probably forgotten, or possibly something she preferred to blank out. These days she would have had no problem getting an abortion, of course, but,' he sighed, 'here I am.'

'My condolences, Mr Smyth. Your mother died tragically. We shall find her killer, I assure you, but any background information you may be able to give will be invaluable. You were familiar with her business contacts?'

He sobered, suddenly looking his age. 'Some. Not all. Lulu – I always called her that, she insisted upon it – entrusted me with certain little errands. I must have inherited her gift for languages, and she found my proven discretion useful too.'

'Your own work took you abroad?'

'I operate a specialized security business guarding celebrities in a discreet way; a fixer, promoting my clients' public profiles when required, burying their indiscretions when called for. I am very good at it,' he said with an engaging smile, and Hayes believed every word.

'It was I who introduced Lulu to a media friend and, of course, she proved to be a natural, an eccentric personality not seen on film since Edith Sitwell in my view,' Rory continued. He paused. 'But there is one matter I need to clear up, chief inspector.

140

The alleged break-in here. Mrs Sharpley was quite right. There was an intruder the other night. It was me.'

Hayes held his tongue, recognizing Smyth's glib delivery as a basic trait, a need to be in control of what, in any other context, might be regarded as a police interrogation.

'Go on.'

'When the news of Lulu's murder was broadcast, I knew I had no time to lose. I let myself in as quietly as I could and searched every inch of this place. It was a long shot; Lulu could have hidden it even. But I doubted that. It was the sort of information she would keep close, to be readily available if she needed to get rid of it at short notice.'

Hayes tensed. 'Illegal transactions?'

Smyth frowned. 'I suppose you could call it that. My inconvenient birth remained a burden all her life. I think she was ashamed to have dumped me as she did. Yes, an illegal transaction you could call it. The adoption certainly never went through the usual channels, although the Smyths made sure it was waterproof, you might say. From brief allusions to her own early life Lulu seemed to have had a happy childhood and when her entire family disappeared in the process of Stalin's Pogroms, throwing away her only remaining blood tie, even if it was a child she neither wanted nor could care for at the time – this was before her marriage, you see, before she had established so much as a toehold in this country – left an enduring feeling of guilt that she spent years trying to forget. I came here to her flat that night to find my birth certificate and any adoption papers. I knew that Mr Ball was doubtful of the blood tie but, apart from that, I needed proof for my own satisfaction.'

'You tidied up the flat, wiped the fingerprints and so on. Why was that?'

'Lulu had left the place in her usual chaos. Just clearing her desk left me with a pile of junk and the other rooms were as bad. Knowing she was never coming back, I couldn't leave it like that, especially the cat litter tray, which starts to stink within days. That was the one way we differed: I'm neat, Lulu's concerned with more important things than housework. I emptied the fridge and left the flat smelling like roses. Now you know why I'm so good at my job, chief inspector. Cleaning up other people's shit is my business.'

Hayes looked across at Bellamy, who shrugged in response.

Rory bent down and unlocked his briefcase, extracting a scuffed manila envelope, and passed it to Hayes. It contained the faded documentation Robert Smyth needed. Hayes flipped through the papers and then returned them without a word.

After a moment's silence he attempted to lower the emotional temperature that Rory's painful recollections had unexpectedly brought to the surface. 'Thank you, Mr Smyth. You are, of course, aware that the gallery was burnt out?'

He shrugged. 'Well insured, I hope. A pity about poor old Musset. Whatever was he doing on the premises?'

'It's not my investigation, Mr Smyth. You will have to contact Inspector Mayhew, who's the man in charge.' He coughed. 'My enquiries are only concerned with your mother's death. Would you be willing to identify the body? Once the formalities are complete you may wish to arrange the funeral. The coroner's decision, I'm afraid, but I hope the delay will be minimal.'

'Yes, of course. When shall I come?'

'I'll ring you, shall I? There are other matters I would like to discuss with you but we can deal with all that at the station, OK?'

'Just one thing. The keys to this flat. May I have them? I understand Mrs Sharpley withdrew her complaint about an intruder. She's relieved,' he added with a note of apology, 'it was only me.'

'Sorry, sir. The keys remain with us at present. I will return them to Mr Ball in due course and then you can settle with him when the legal niceties are covered. Do you have keys to the gallery?'

'No, Lulu kept that side of her life to herself. Musset had keys of course but as far as I am aware that was it.'

Hayes nodded and jumped to his feet, anxious to conclude the interview before Smyth dug into more sentimental rot about his mother and her alleged feelings of guilt. Hayes personally thought this all baloney but who was he to judge? Bellamy opened the front door, waiting for Rory to collect his coat and briefcase. The three men stood in the dimly lit corridor, crowding the narrow space as they discussed arrangements for Smyth's attendance at the mortuary.

After locking up Hayes and Bellamy strolled to the lift, leaving the sad, grey-haired man in the camel coat to return to the comfort of Mrs Sharpley's tea and sympathy.

Eighteen

It was Saturday afternoon before Jenny Robbins was able to get hold of Tessa Cox.

'We've only just got home. Is it really necessary to take my statement *now*?'

'I'm afraid so. You found the body, Mrs Cox. Your accurate recollection of events is important for the investigation and almost a week's gone by already. We could insist that you come to the station, you know, and the superintendent's not best pleased that the paperwork's all behind schedule. Your co-operation would be much appreciated.'

Jenny Robbins resented the note of pleading that had crept in, but Tessa Cox's manner was brusque and a softly-softly approach was probably best.

'Well, all right. I'll get on with the unpacking. It won't take long, will it? My husband's just off to Alexei's school to pick him up after his skiing trip. We were looking forward to a quiet weekend.'

Aren't we all? Jenny silently retorted, but

kept her flash response to herself, well aware that her short fuse had landed her in trouble before.

She arrived at Woolpack Farm just as it was getting dark. Tessa Cox invited her in, the lofty beamed hall dominated by a huge Christmas tree as yet undecorated. Her manner was cool, the few days away with her husband evidently damping down the trauma of finding Lulu Starewska's body. Jenny wondered about that work Tessa had claimed was so urgent before the return of her nine-year-old stepson.

Tessa Cox wore a holly-red tracksuit that complimented her pale skin and dark, curly hair. Jenny had never chosen to wear scarlet herself, her own flaming locks inhibiting any antics with bright outfits. While she waited for Tessa to put on all the lights, she idly explored the possibility of branching out from the safe sub-fusc colours she had got used to. Tessa Cox was a professional artist, wasn't she? And colour didn't faze her, judging by the eye-bending saffron paint-work of the hall that, as she discovered as she followed Tessa into the sitting room, led to a terracotta décor enlivened with several starkly abstract pictures slashed with swathes of black and gold.

'Tony likes a dramatic effect,' Tessa said with a rueful grin. 'My parents would have had a fit, their own DIY limited to magnolia walls and tasteful prints. But when Tony agreed to live here it seemed only fair to let him put his own stamp on the place. Do sit down. Tea?'

'No, thanks.' Jenny perched on one of the sofas and produced a folder. 'If we could rough out a statement, you could sign it straight away and I can get out from under your feet. You've been away? We tried to reach you but there was no contact number.'

'We stayed in town for a break. The Berkeley. Tony had a couple of business meetings and I did some shopping.'

'You heard about the Star Gallery being fire-bombed?'

Tessa looked up, alarm flaring in the dark eyes, and Jenny mentally applauded, her apparently throw-away comment clearly hitting the bull's eye.'

'Fire-bombed? Surely not. An accident, faulty wiring or something.'

'Mr Musset was killed.'

Tessa jumped up and poured herself a stiff whisky, in shock her natural courtesy abandoning her. Jenny relaxed, content that the assumed veneer of self-confidence was only skin deep. She let it ride, insisting that her reluctant witness got to grips with the matter in hand. After juggling with Cox's recollections of the fatal Sunday afternoon, and prompted by Jenny's pertinent questions, a statement was hammered out and signed.

They moved to the door just as Tony Cox burst in, erupting into the room like a typhoon, his fleshy jowls flushed with temper. He ignored Jenny, rushing at Tessa and gripping her shoulders with shaking hands.

'He's gone, Tess. Alexei's been kidnapped. That bitch Vera's whisked him from right under the nose of that stupid teacher.'

'Vera was at the school? Got there before you arrived?'

'No, worse. She was waiting at Arrivals at Heathrow. Walked straight up to that silly cow, Mrs Edwards, handed her a letter supposedly signed by me which said we would be unable to pick up Alexei as arranged and that he was to go with his mother who would be waiting at the airport with appropriate identification. Vera said she had arranged with us to take Alexei home for Christmas!'

'And they let her take him?'

'Alexei was thrilled to see his mother, they said. Insisted it was all right and was gabbling away in Russian like a bloody little "Trot". And when the Edwards woman took him aside and asked him, "Do you want to go with this lady?" he was pleased as punch, hugged Vera and clung on till they gave in. "What else were we to do, Mr Cox?" they said. "We tried ringing you at home to confirm the arrangement but there was no answer." A real fuck-up.'

'So they just let him go with that crazy creature?' Tessa snapped.

'Let her collect his baggage and, worst of all, handed over his passport. The kid could be anywhere by now. Vera could have booked them straight on a flight to Europe there and then, a good two hours' grace before I turned up to collect Alexei from the school here as arranged. I'll sue the bloody lot of them. Christ Almighty, Tess, what are we going to do?'

Jenny pushed forward and produced her ID card. 'You must call the police straight away, Mr Cox. We can warn all the ports and exits to arrest the kidnapper. Was she alone, the boy's mother?'

'A man ... A man was with her, they said. He didn't get involved in this exchange at the Arrivals Lounge but he definitely took charge of the bags, the skis and stuff.'

'And your son was happy with this change

of plan?'

'Over the moon, apparently. He hasn't seen his mother for nearly a year. Contact is minimal and meetings are supervised owing to the restrictions the court imposed. There was never a possibility of a home stay, Vera knows that. I'll have her banged up for life after this, the crazy bitch.'

'But the school knew nothing of any visiting restrictions?'

Tony Cox turned on Robbins, all guns blazing. 'No, of course they bloody didn't. Why would I discuss my private life with a fucking school teacher? Alexei's been with us for three years, Vera's a clapped-out nutter, how could I possibly imagine she'd pull a stunt like this?'

'Does your son have a mobile phone?'

'Yes,' Tessa quietly agreed. 'I think he used to ring his mother at weekends. They spoke in Russian. I occasionally overheard a little of the conversation but it seemed cruel to cut him off completely from his mother. He lived with her for the first five or six years of his life. He loved her.'

'You said nothing to me about this!' he bawled, his unbridled anger fizzing in the air. Tessa lowered her gaze and took a step back.

'Your ex-wife must have known all about

Alexei's skiing trip then, Mr Cox?'

'Probably,' he admitted.

'Well, let's get moving,' Jenny directed, stuffing his wife's statement in her notebook and putting out an emergency alert to the station.

Hayes arrived like the cavalry, his tyres burning skid marks in the raked gravel of the drive. Jenny Robbins set about keeping the Coxes under surveillance, terribly afraid that the death of an old woman had spread like a stain, now enveloping a nine-year-old child.

Nineteen

After hearing out a more restrained account of the abduction from Tony Cox, Hayes insisted on calling in Superintendent Waller. The possible kidnap of a young boy was real headline stuff and Hayes was reluctant to set the firepower of a possible international search in motion without sanction from the big boys.

Tony Cox was impatient with the delay, demanding an immediate police response, the arrest of the poor benighted school teacher at the very least. Jenny Robbins tried to calm things down but with the added presence of Sergeant Bellamy the sitting room of Woolpack Farm quickly assumed the atmosphere of a full-blown panic station. Waller's swift arrival was a relief all round; nothing like passing the buck when the stakes were this high, Hayes acknowledged. A murder investigation was bad enough, but a bloody kidnapping charge was dynamite. Were the two disasters connected, he wondered? At least the death of Musset was conveniently in the Met's court.

Waller was, in fact, at his best in a situation like this. He suggested they all sit down to listen to yet another re-run of Cox's story. Tessa had withdrawn to a window seat, her anxiety masked by a strange reluctance to back up her husband's distress. Jenny watched her with interest. The boy was Tessa's stepchild, of course, and had lived with them at the farm for only the past three years, but there was something else she could not quite put her finger on. There was a definite coldness about the woman's reactions, a backing-off from the current drama as if Tessa Cox was determined to distance herself from this, the latest disaster in a three act tragedy; first Starewska, secondly Musset and now a missing boy. Was she hiding something, Jenny wondered, or just callous?

'Now, have I got this straight, Mr Cox?' Waller insisted. 'Your ex-wife is not sectioned or under any psychiatric restriction, merely required to see her son under supervision and with your permission? And this arrangement has worked well since you gained custody of the boy?'

Cox nodded. 'Vera was suffering from a

mental condition that deluded her into thinking the KGB – or the Russian mafia, I'm not sure which – was trying to kill her, to poison her food and so on. We parted soon after Alexei was born and I work abroad a good deal and so the crazy nightmare she had concocted remained undetected until Alexei was due to start school. My ex is Russian, of course, and came to live in the UK only after considerable bureaucratic visa nonsense following our marriage.

'She spoke little English at first and found living in a strange country frightening. Alexei was born in London but it would seem the two of them led a very secluded existence, seeing no one. The child slept in the same bed as his mother right up until I gained custody and brought him to live here with us. A social worker had discovered that Alexei's diet had been rigorously restricted, owing to Vera's paranoia that Russian agents were out to poison her and her child. Alexei was seriously underweight, spoke no English, and Vera refused to allow him out of her sight even to go to school. The authorities were also concerned about him sleeping with her but no sexual interference was proved. I had just got married at that time and after Vera had been taken into residential care for treatment, the court allowed the boy to come to live with us.'

'But your ex-wife got better and was released into the community?'

'She has a flat. There is a certain amount of supervision and Alexei was permitted to visit her in the company of a social worker roughly every three months but this has lapsed. Vera was never allowed to be alone with him.'

'But she is sane enough to live alone?' Waller barked.

'I suppose so. I haven't seen her myself for at least three years.'

'And your son is happy with the current arrangement; living here, going to school locally?'

'Absolutely.'

Waller beckoned Hayes to join him in the hall and closed the door. 'Bloody rum do, Hayes. What do you make of it?'

'Frankly, sir, I wouldn't go so far as to call it a kidnapping. The kid was glad to go with his mother, there was no reluctance according to Mrs Edwards, the school teacher in charge. Who was she to insist the boy was only to be picked up by his father when they got back to the school, where all the parents were due to collect their kids? If this Mrs Edwards was handed a letter allegedly from

Cox stating that he and his wife were detained and there was a change of plan, she had little option but to comply. The child was to be given into the safe keeping of his mother who would formally identify herself. The teacher tried getting confirmation from Cox but he was not at home, so she let it go. The chances were if she ignored the letter and insisted on returning him to the school with the rest of the party, there'd be all hell to pay if the parents were away and there was no one at home to care for him. The mother, Vera, had all the trump cards, and if a forged letter is in the game the snatch was extremely well organized and hardly the single-handed work of an alleged nutter.

'We shall have to confirm all this with the school, of course, but in Cox's shoes I'd try to settle this quietly. A national outcry can only distress the boy and chances are Vera got fed up with the way her access was restricted and decided to take a chance. If she's a nice-looking woman who only wants to have her son to stay for Christmas, the press will jump on the bandwagon and accuse us of criminalizing the poor bitch. You know how mawkish the tabloids get if a sob story like that gets an airing.'

'Has the Cox bloke tried ringing her at home?'

'Not as far as I know. Let's try to cool it, sir. Persuade Cox to see what we can find out without calling out the bloodhounds.'

Waller nodded. 'Send Robbins off to see this school teacher and we'll try to keep the lid on it as long as possible.'

When they returned to the sitting room Cox had disappeared.

Bellamy approached Hayes and whispered, 'He got a phone call, sir. Took it in his study. Said it was a business call, nothing to do with the missing lad.'

Tessa remained seated in the window seat, trancelike, her eyes closed. Hayes insisted on locating her husband and dragged him back to confer with the boss. The man looked utterly drained, his cheeks now grey, the fleshy folds of his face etched in deep furrows adding years to the man.

Waller summarized the plan of action; a discreet dragnet, just an alert at all points of exit to apprehend Vera Cox and her son Alexei on an unspecified security alert.

'They won't get far, sir,' Waller assured him. 'And, in the meantime, you could make a few phone calls yourself. Advise the person supervising your ex-wife's welfare that there's been a misunderstanding about a Christmas visit but you are making no charges provided the boy is returned immediately.'

'What if he's not found over the weekend?' Tessa put in.

'Then we shall have to take more drastic steps. But the poor woman isn't going to harm the boy, is she? We don't want to panic her into going underground. Any idea who this man friend of hers is, Mr Cox?'

He miserably shook his head and, after a further reiteration of the plan of action, Waller departed, leaving Hayes and his sergeant to cool the situation. Jenny Robbins was despatched to track down the school teacher and get a statement, and Bellamy was to stay put and monitor any incoming calls.

'Don't take any flak from Cox or his wife,' Hayes warned. 'I'm going back to the station to set the ball rolling. I guarantee this kid'll be tucked up with his mum at her flat by now. Prising the poor little sod off the nest is going to be tricky but let's hope this Russian woman's not as barmy as Cox claims.'

Twenty

All leave was cancelled. Waller took charge of the search for Alexei Cox and made up a team, including Jenny Robbins, each officer under strict orders to keep the alleged kidnapping top secret. Waller was, Hayes decided, the ideal one to deal with Tony Cox, his abrasive approach brooking no nonsense from the boy's father

The plan was to flush out Vera Cox and her child without publicity, only televising pictures of the two if, after twenty-four hours, the unfortunate woman had not been found. The boyfriend in the background might present problems because from what they gathered about Vera Cox she was never in a position to effect an abduction without help. But in Waller's mind calling it an abduction was well over the top. Knowing the snail-like pace of social workers it might well be that Vera Cox's mental breakdown was a thing of the past and yet, from a mother's point of view, reversing a court decision would be all but impossible. The boy had settled down in his new home, was happy at school, now spoke excellent English and was likely to enjoy a comfortable lifestyle in a wealthy home with a loving father.

Waller relished the task ahead, confident of his ability to sidestep the legal hurdles and return the boy to Woolpack Farm with no harm done.

Hayes considered the strength of his reduced squad, Waller having claimed the lion's share to deal with the Cox emergency. To be fair, Hayes had to admit, the whereabouts of a small boy was infinitely more important than the death of an old woman. Even so, a killer was at large and progress was slow.

Hayes drove back to the village to assess the situation and found only a scratch team still at work in the mobile incident room on the Green. He left Bellamy to go through a batch of reports and crossed the road to let himself into Star Cottage.

The place was cold as charity, the off-peak heating having little effect on the December chill factor. He put on the lights and stood in the sitting room, trying to imagine Lulu Starewska at home here. It was cosier than the flat in St Bede's Square but the old lady had certainly been no natural homemaker. He took a slow excursion round the house, examining each room with care, trying to spot something, anything, to throw some light on the mystery.

The bedroom was sparsely furnished, the dressing table littered with pots of make-up and a drawer full of spent lipsticks and clutter. From the photographs in the press following the murder, one could see the ravages of time had not entirely eliminated an undeniable glamour, a hard-edged thirties style that had made her unique. The old girl had been heavy on the cosmetics and bizarre in her choice of flowing garments and chunky jewellery, but Hayes guessed this extraordinary façade was no camouflage. Lulu Starewska had chosen this flamboyant style from the start and courageously gave no quarter to the passing years.

He retraced his steps and spent fifteen minutes in the kitchen, rekindling the details of the crime scene; the tumbled tablecloth, the pools of blood and spattered walls, the crumpled body clutching, even in her death throes, at the auburn wig.

A rap at the door broke into his reverie and he hurried to see what had brought one of the team to fetch him so quickly. But it wasn't any policeman. It was Dolly Froude.

'I saw a light, I thought I'd better check,' she said, smiling with relief to find it was only Hayes.

'You thought one of the village yobs had broken in?'

'Not really. They're a superstitious lot, wary of a place likely to be spooky. But on the whole they're good lads and they liked Lulu. She stood up for them when that petition was doing the rounds. Would you like to come back for a drink, inspector? It's bloody freezing in here.'

'Yes, that'd be good. I was just having a quiet look round, hoping for inspiration to strike,' he said ruefully. 'I'll just lock up and be right with you.'

Dolly had made some sandwiches and a pot of coffee by the time he had shut up Star Cottage. The place was a welcome contrast, a fire crackling in the grate, curtains drawn against a bitter fall in temperature.

'Feels like snow to me,' she said as she took his coat. 'And to think that only a week ago poor Lulu was here, enjoying her Saturday night play on the radio. Couldn't be bothered with the telly but loved the "wireless", as she called it. She could get all her foreign programmes, you see, the World Service and stations broadcasting from

Europe. She was such a clever woman, inspector. My partner, Joyce, thought the world of her. "So brave," Joyce used to say to me, "Lulu's fighting the whole world, not giving an inch."'

Hayes settled by the fire and accepted a plate of sandwiches and a mug of coffee laced with a slug of brandy. He felt at ease with Dolly Froude, a no-nonsense sort untrammelled by the difficulties of living in a small community where gossip spiced the humdrum rhythm of year on year of the same people going about their same old lives.

'You will miss Mrs Starewska.'

'And how! Joyce gone and now Lulu. It will never be the same. She hardly ever missed her weekends here, you know. Friday night she'd give a toot on the horn to let us know she was back, park the car, let the cat out into the lane, and settle down for a nice rest. No visitors except Joyce or me popping in for a chat, though recently Tessa Cox occasionally dropped by. Didn't stay long, just checking up that Lulu was OK, I suppose.'

'No one else? No men?'

'Men? Oh, you mean Tony Cox. No, Tony didn't bother to call. If he was in England he mostly booked a hotel room in London all week, so I heard, so any business with Lulu could be dealt with in town, couldn't it? No, Star Cottage was her refuge, only very special friends crossed the threshold.'

'Not even her son?'

Dolly started up, wide-eyed. 'Lulu had a son? You're joking! I don't believe it.'

'On my honour, Dolly. Lulu's secret. She kept Rory's existence totally off the record for sixty years at least. He was adopted, goes by the name of Robert Smyth, but stayed in touch on the understanding he never told anyone of the relationship. You'll probably meet him. Rory's inherited everything, including the cottage.'

Dolly topped up her coffee with a booster from the brandy bottle and poised it over Hayes' mug.

He shook his head. 'Double shock for the guy. Losing his mother like that and then the gallery.'

'Yes, I heard. The manager lost his life in the fire, I gather. Terrible tragedy. Will this son of hers rebuild the business?'

'I doubt it. The manager was an expert and most of the stock was destroyed. It would be almost impossible to start up again even if Mr Smyth was interested, which I don't think he is. He has a business of his own and trading stuff like Mrs

Starewska specialized in would take a connoisseur. Tell me something, Dolly. Did your neighbour regularly leave her door unlatched? Mrs Cox says it was always open. Seems strange to me.'

Dolly relaxed, lighting up a foul-smelling cigarello and inviting Hayes to join her. He brought out his cigarettes and waited for her answer.

'Well, yes and no. Lulu didn't bother to lock the front door all day. The cottage was in clear view from the Green and right by the bus stop so in daylight there were plenty of people about, and Lulu never left the cottage at weekends. She brought her shopping with her and didn't shop in the village, which some thought was snobby but it wasn't. Lulu just liked to stay put. In the summer she sometimes sat in the garden but once the days drew in she enjoyed her own company and apart from Joyce and myself made no friends in Bartram.'

'But the door was always open for people to drop by? The lads from the bus shelter, for instance? Did she ever let them into the house?'

'Good God, no! She got on well with the boys but, like I say, Lulu preferred her privacy. She locked the door at night, of course. As soon as it got dark as I recall. You think she let in her killer? It was someone she knew?'

'Well, there was no break-in, for sure. It's the most likely scenario, isn't it? Even someone as brave as your Joyce thought her to be would be foolish to open the door to a stranger at night.'

'Lulu was streetwise, she had lived in the city all her life, confident enough to relax in the cottage but not stupid. She was an old woman, inspector, even if she didn't admit it to herself. With all the terrible things we hear about on the news, even Lulu wouldn't admit anyone after dark, unless, of course, it was that son of hers. Fancy that! I can hardly believe it, keeping him to herself all these years.'

Hayes rose to go, thanking her for the welcome break. 'Oh, and thank you very much for dealing with the cat. The vet was very helpful as it happens. We were able to identify the acid used. It's recovering, I hear.'

'Pushkin's still at the vet's but will probably be re-homed quite soon. With my work taking me away for weeks at a time, keeping a cat is awkward. The woman at the post office said she'd take him on and I've made arrangements with the vet to continue to bill me for any future expenses.'

'You've been very kind, Dolly. Let me know if you think of anything that might help us clear up this case. Thanks for the coffee.'

Hayes made his way back to the mobile incident unit and, after detailing two men to keep an eye on Star Cottage overnight, dismissed the team and told Bellamy to scale down the rota over the weekend. 'We're not going to apprehend any killer round here, lads. I've checked the cottage again; there's nothing of value and I'm hoping to pass it on to the solicitor next week and let him make suitable security arrangements. With the superintendent taking half our squad for his own investigation we haven't the manpower to keep a permanent watch on the premises.'

The men gladly shut their files and trooped out, everyone all but wiped out by a long day. Bellamy was the last to leave and approached Hayes with a cheerfulness that did nothing to lift the gloom.

'Good news, sir. A breakthrough. DC Roper tracked down the motor boat. *"Stargazer"*. Hired from a small firm in Oxford. Bloke paid by credit card, a man called Kuvrov.'

Hayes leapt up, hope glinting in his weary eyes like a foretaste of Christmas. He slammed his fist into the door with a shout of exultation. 'At last!'

'That was the good news, sir. The bad news is this guy Kuvrov's claimed diplomatic immunity. He's not available for questioning – in fact, he's skipped the country.'

Twenty-one

It was after eight o'clock on Saturday night before Jenny Robbins located Vera Cox's social worker, a patient woman who greeted Robbins' arrival on her doorstep on her first weekend off since November with weary resignation. Marie O'Connor had been at the job too long to insist on union hours and invited Jenny to come inside.

The house was small and meticulously tidy, no evidence of any other members of the family there at all. Mrs O'Connor was, Jenny decided, well on the way to retirement, her grey hair tied back in an elastic band, her generous proportions comfortably draped in a colourful kaftan.

'Come in, dear, I expect you're cold. I'll put the kettle on, shall I?'

Jenny decided that if ever she was put on a social worker's hit list, Marie O'Connor was the lady she'd be hoping for. Unhurried. Unflappable. Kind. Marie turned off the television and bustled about making tea, passing Jenny a dainty cup and saucer, a nice touch, and clearly not best china for any official visit but an everyday little luxury.

'Now, what can I do for you?'

Jenny described the apparent abduction of Alexei Cox and the superintendent's decision to try to find the boy without publicity for twenty-four hours at least. 'Can you tell me about Vera Cox, Mrs O'Connor? Her ex seems to think she is unbalanced and that Alexei is in danger.'

'Oh no, certainly not. Vera adores that child. She's not even on medication any longer. I've been trying to persuade her to apply for more access but Vera's terrified of the authorities; the police, the courts and especially her doctors. Poor soul doesn't understand that we're not living in a police state, that she's entitled to ask for a better deal but is frightened of her husband, who is rich and powerful, I understand. And so she gets no further. Snatching the boy at the airport was very stupid and will do her case no good at all. You say she had help?'

'A man was with her. We've tried her flat; there's no answer. It is imperative we find her straight away, Mrs O'Connor. If the boy is not returned to his father by Monday morning, my boss will make it official, put her picture out and possibly ruin her last chance to be with her son.'

'Vera has been on my list for the past two years. She has suffered, poor thing, her delusions starting as post-natal depression, which escalated into a terrible food phobia. Because she spoke little English at first and claimed no benefits, she just slipped through the net. It was only when the child was due to start school that the extent of her paranoia was exposed.'

'Mr Cox says Vera thought the Russian secret police were trying to kill her.'

'He did? Well, perhaps that's true, I only came on the scene when she was discharged from hospital. Vera's a timid soul and no threat to anyone. You think she had help? A boyfriend? First I've heard of it. Might be someone she met at work. I got her a little part-time job in the summer. Check-out girl at a supermarket. She's really very bright and, given time, she will come off my list and be able to get on with her life. She's only thirty-two, much younger than that husband of hers, who didn't look after her at all if you ask me. Left her to sink or swim in a strange city with a baby to look after and no family around.'

'Mr Cox has a new wife, another younger woman. She seems quite fond of Alexei.'

'Good. Well, we must see what we can do. You've been to the flat, you say, and got no answer. I've got a key somewhere – Vera was a potential suicide at one time. Would you like me to come with you, see if we can get some idea where's she's gone or even if she's just lying low in the flat? I haven't seen her this month, work gets very busy in my department in the run-up to Christmas.'

'Would it be worth speaking to her boss at the supermarket? Without leaking any information about the reason for the police enquiry, of course. We don't want to spoil her chances at work.'

Marie O'Connor made a few phone calls and they decided to use her car. 'I know my way round here and the supermarket manager trusts me. A sensible man, takes one or two of my clients every year, gives these sad people a fresh start, not that it always works out, but we try. We try,' she added with a smile.

The supermarket was almost closing, the place still heaving with last-minute shoppers, carols trilling from loudspeakers, every aisle jammed with boxes of Christmas crackers, candles and glitzy tree decorations kicked aside by exhausted shelf stackers.

The manager ushered them into his office, courteous but clearly harassed, anxious to be home and off the premises for a decent hour's relaxation. Jenny left Marie to sketch an outline of the problem, making Vera's disappearance sound like a bank holiday jaunt rather than a possible kidnapping.

Jenny decided to sharpen the tone. 'Did Vera make any friends at work that you know of, Mr Patel? Anyone who knew she was planning to have her son to stay with her for the Christmas holidays?'

He shrugged. 'Not that I know. I'll speak to the staff supervisor, see if she's got an idea.'

After half an hour and a blank response from the supervisor, Jenny knew it was hopeless. Vera seemed to have made little impact at work. She was a good timekeeper, reliable, had mastered the till with no problem at all and seemed quiet but cheerful. No friends, though. No one to share a coffee with at break-time, no one calling to collect her at the end of her shift.

They drove round to Vera's flat, which was only a short bus ride away and situated on an estate by the river. While Marie went inside to search for a clue as to Vera's whereabouts, Jenny knocked up the neighbours, spinning a plausible line about Vera's non-appearance at work and the anxiety of her social worker regarding her state of mind.

A young black woman with a toddler clinging to her skirt was the most forthcoming. 'Christmas is a lonely time for single mums,' she admitted. 'You don't think Vera's topped herself, do you? It's the bloody season for it, you know. Miserable weather, no money, every other bugger having fun, going to parties. Stands to reason Vera missed her kid. You tried that boyfriend of hers? They might have bunked off for a visit with their foreign friends.'

'You've met the boyfriend?'

'Not exactly, but I've seen him around the place. Big bloke, didn't seem to feel the cold or perhaps he just wanted to show off his tattoos. Never wore much more than a T-shirt even when it was pissing down.'

'And tattooed, you say? Anything special? Dragons, snakes? The usual stuff?'

'No. I knocked at Vera's door the other night to borrow some tea bags. I'd run out, see, and though she don't say much, Vera's all heart, wouldn't turn away a beggar in the street. Like I was saying, this foreign bloke, another refugee, I bet, come to her door, all bare up top he was, just got out of the bath by the look of his hair. A real muscle man. Looked a bit of a bruiser to me, not my type. Vera ought to be careful, guys like that can get rough. But what really knocked me sideways was seeing his chest covered with all them tattoos. Religious stuff, Madonna and Child with a fairy castle in the background. Like Disneyland it was, nothing like the Chinese stuff biker boys go in for.'

'He wasn't English, you say. Russian, like Vera?'

'Probably. How would I know? But foreign all right.'

'And this fairy castle tattoo on his chest. Did it have domes like onions?'

'Yeah, that's it! Stripy onions. All colours. But religious, too. Some sort of Hari Krisna mob, d'you think?'

Jenny gave the woman her card and made a note of her name. Bernice Baker. Bernice promised to give her a ring if Vera turned up.

'She's not in any trouble, Bernice. We just want to make sure she's all right.'

She hurried back to Vera's flat just as Marie was locking up.

'No one there, duck. No letters, no travel brochures. Nothing in the fridge for a kid to eat.'

'Does Vera have a phone in the flat?'

'No. Couldn't afford it, she said. But she used to get calls from her son at weekends so she must have had a mobile. Didn't give me the number, though, didn't want a nosy parker like me checking up on her at work, I suppose, and I don't like to press my luck. Gaining a client's confidence is difficult enough; get too pushy and you've lost her for good. Any lead on this boyfriend?'

Jenny gave her a run-down on her conversation with the woman next door and they agreed to call it a day.

'I'll pop round and check with Bernice tomorrow night. Bernice Baker, you said? She might remember something else; and without being rude, Jenny, talking to the fuzz – even nice-looking young girls like you – doesn't always get to the bottom line.'

Marie dropped Jenny back at the house to pick up her car, and Jenny then phoned through to Waller to get further instructions.

'Stay where you are, Robbins. Book into a B&B nearby and knock up more of the neighbours in the morning. Ask any kids who are hanging about on the estate if they've seen this foreign bloke. Kids see everything that goes on in a place like that, a weirdo tattooed like the bloody Sistine Chapel wouldn't have gone unnoticed.'

When Hayes phoned through to Waller and filled him in with the news that one of the men seen by Darren down by the river had been identified as an untouchable, a man with diplomatic immunity, Waller took it surprisingly philosophically.

'Let's not jump to conclusions, Hayes. We may have lost this Kuvrov guy but his bully boy, a tattooed git seen with Vera Cox, is still in the frame. No sighting of either of them or the boy at any exit point. They're holed up somewhere safe but a threesome like that's bound to break cover before long and they'll be spotted. I'll hold my fire till Monday morning and if we're no further forward by then we'll put the missing kid on every news broadcast in the country.'

Twenty-two

Robert Smyth phoned Hayes on Sunday morning to ask if he could see his mother's body that afternoon. 'Sorry to bother you at the weekend, inspector, but I'd like to pay my respects before she is transferred to the undertakers.'

'No problem, Mr Smyth. I'm on duty this weekend in any case and I'd like to get your formal identification on record. Shall we say two o'clock?' Hayes gave Rory directions and got back to work.

Escorting relatives to view their loved ones, especially those like Lulu Starewska, whose battered features could not be disguised, was not favourite for a Sunday afternoon but, as his own plans had been scuppered and Pippa had flounced off to spend the weekend with her sister in Swansea, Hayes was free to concentrate on the investigation.

Robert Smyth breezed in to greet Hayes in the all too familiar waiting room. A tall and apparently athletic man, Lulu's prodigal son was really nothing to be ashamed of. He wore his camel overcoat with a certain panache and with his well-groomed looks and a subtle aftershave to top it off Rory could be mistaken for a diplomat. Hayes put a private wager on Rory's fingernails being manicured, too, and only just stopped himself from taking a closer gander at the man's hands as he took off his coat and laid it on an empty chair.

The room was close and Hayes noticed a film of sweat glistening on Rory's forehead. Perhaps he had been too cynical, perhaps Lulu's son was genuinely cut up about her death, but, whether he was or not, Hayes felt obliged to spell out the usual warnings about witnesses preparing themselves for the ordeal.

In fact, Rory took it well, the perceptive stiffening of his relaxed posture as the mortuary attendant pulled back the sheet being the only sign of shock. Lulu's face would be a shock to anyone, the damaged features of an old woman enough to strike fear in the heart of even the staunchest witness. Rory nodded and turned away and Hayes escorted him back to the waiting room to pick up his coat.

They stood on the steps outside the

mortuary, sheltering under the portico, Rory having said not a word since they viewed the corpse.

'I wonder if I might presume on your time for a little longer, inspector? I'm a member of a private drinking club nearby. It's quiet at weekends and I feel the need of some company.'

Hayes readily agreed, hoping to pin Smyth down over some baffling problems about the gallery fire.

'Sure. Why not?'

The club was only a five-minute walk away. 'A hangover from my bad old days,' Rory admitted. 'When carousing the night away was all too frequent. I managed to kick the habit but kept up my membership to test my resolve, I suppose, and the members are a nice bunch, mostly interesting, and by no means restricted to the university crowd. Oxford does have a commercial life, too, an aspect of living here that tourists never seem to grasp. But I must be boring you, inspector. I'm sure you're all too familiar with the gown versus town argument.'

'I was attached to the police in Oxford for several years. Transferring to Renham is relatively recent.'

'Not so wild, I imagine.'

'Actually, a country patch harbours as

much, if not more, crime than the city. Can't think why, but we've had our share of excitement since I moved to the sticks.'

The club was in the basement of a hotel and proved to be a pleasant retreat from the wet streets outside. Leather armchairs and dim lighting gave the drinkers the cosy assurance that boozing the afternoon away was perfectly acceptable. In fact, there were a few still hanging on after lunch, and a low hum of conversation spiked with the occasional guffaw made Rory's choice of venue a welcome break after the bleak atmosphere of the mortuary.

Rory ordered a bottle of wine and they settled at a corner table. He seemed to have recovered from the shock of seeing Lulu so brutally attacked but refrained from mentioning it, anxious, in Hayes' view, to regain his composure.

They talked instead about the fire.

'The local inspector called me in to discuss my own movements on Friday. Perfectly civil, but he is required to explore every possible motive, of course. A chap called Detective Inspector Mayhew.'

'Yes, I met him.'

'Though why I should fire-bomb what was, in effect, my own property seems strange.'

'Perhaps he thought you might be more interested in the insurance.'

'Do you think so?' Rory shrugged, perplexed by the turn the investigation seemed to be taking and anxious to have Hayes' opinion. 'The inspector asked me if Musset had any enemies. Apart from myself, of course! As Lulu's beneficiary he seemed to imply I was prime suspect. But how would I know about Musset's enemies? I rarely met the man.'

'But you were familiar with the trade. Your mother confided in you, I'm sure, shared business secrets she wanted to keep from Musset.' This was a flyer, Hayes had to admit, but worth a try. It was unlikely he would be in such an informal situation with Robert again.

Smyth's frank response seemed perfectly genuine. 'Oh yes, Lulu found me useful enough. I travel abroad myself and speak Russian so it was not inconvenient to occasionally undertake little errands for her. As my relationship was never revealed to any of her business contacts I managed to act as her secret agent, you might say.'

'Did you keep an eye on Tony Cox? I was informed that Mrs Starewska partly financed his operation in Moscow. Star Motors.'

'I made some checks through my own

contacts, though I made sure Tony Cox was never aware of it. You are quite right. My mother did set him up. It was easy for her and handy at the time. Lulu had money stranded in Russia that was impossible to transfer back to the UK. Financing the garages was one way of maximizing her investment in a perfectly legal way. No call for money laundering, inspector, if that is what's bothering you.'

'And the partnership was fruitful?'

'Most certainly. Lulu had the Midas touch, could recognize a potential gold-mine without any financial advisers pulling strings. There are such people who make a living setting up shell companies to hide Russian oil millions around the world. A dangerous career, and if secrets leak out rich people don't like it when their wealth is flung across newspaper headlines; although purchasing a dacha or a holiday home in Sardinia is increasingly common these days. Material success in, say, St Petersburg, is shown in a sequence of predictable moves. First you buy a Mercedes or a BMW, then it's jewellery and designer clothes, then it goes haywire after that.

'Lulu forecast the demand for luxury cars and Tony Cox was the sort she felt she could manipulate. He was an experienced car salesman and had the flair to put it across. The business flourished. Did you read about that twenty-four-year-old rouble billionaire who bought out one of the last few British sports car manufacturers purely because he fancied himself driving a flashy soft-top? I've even heard of newly rich members of the Moscow jet set buying themselves a fleet of luxury limos when they can't even drive! No, my friend, Lulu had an eye for a money-spinner and helping to set up Tony Cox seemed a good idea at the time.'

'But the partnership soured?'

'Cox got greedy. Started trading on his own. Made some dodgy friends and got involved in a bit of smuggling. Lulu found out, of course, and sent me out there to put a stop to it. I was allegedly there as her "accountant", but tackling Cox was like mud wrestling. She decided to pull him out and told him so by phone.'

'Then she died?'

'Murdered. Let's call it by its proper name, inspector. Tortured and murdered. It doesn't get worse than that,' he said, swigging down his wine and refilling their glasses.

Hayes backed off, anxious to keep things on an even keel. 'You seem to know the ropes, Mr Smyth. Ever heard of a diplomat called Kuvrov?'

Rory shook his head. 'Russian?'

'I think so. Works with a minder sporting spectacular tattoos all over his chest and arms.'

He perked up. 'You don't say. Phew. You think Cox got himself involved with these guys?'

'No proof of it. Just a line of enquiry we're pursuing.'

'Any description of these tattoos?'

'Religious. Madonna and Child with possibly a Russian church or palace in the background.'

'There was a history of these designs in Russian labour camps. Boys who were children of "enemies of the people", who were later put to work as guards in these camps. The tattoos became badges of honour within a criminal class obliged to take the only work open to them as tools of the authorities, doling out punishments and recognizable by the "uniform" of their skin designs. A depiction of the Virgin, a rough copy of images one sees on icons, is common. The background varies but onion domes and orthodox symbols are often used, which is extraordinary considering the vicious activities this underclass is called upon to perform. Dirty work. Sad in a way. These men were doomed from the start and now that the camps are largely disbanded they are working for the mafia.'

This fascinating insight was rudely interrupted by Hayes' mobile phone. Several drinkers peevishly looked up. He apologized to his host. Rory grinned and gave the thumbs up to the barman, who was presumably under orders to silence all mobile phones in case the intrusion of the big bad world outside crept in.

Hayes listened intently to the office on the other end of his mobile then quickly rose to his feet. 'I must go. It's been very interesting, Mr Smyth. Perhaps we could continue this another time?'

'Duty calls?'

'Urgent.' He paused then dived in regardless. 'This is strictly confidential, Mr Smyth, but as an interested party perhaps you should know that Tony Cox has disappeared. Left a message with his wife to cut off the police search for his son.'

'Alexei's missing?'

'Cox's ex-wife snatched the child from a school party yesterday. We've been keeping it under wraps but, according to Tessa Cox, they've negotiated a private deal.'

'Blackmail?'

'What makes you say that?'

'Obvious, I would have thought. The boy is kidnapped, no pay-off is demanded – am I right? But Cox arranges an exchange without involving the police.'

'But the phones have been monitored and there was no ransom note.'

'In that case Cox knew what was required without it being spelt out. Cox has crossed the line and if he's disappeared he won't be seen again until the price is paid.'

'Tessa is picking up the kid from a place that will only be designated once Tony Cox has made the drop, I presume. She says the ex-wife trusts her and Alexei will be less traumatized if his father's not there to start a fight with the boy's mother. But how would he get the money together immediately on a Sunday? She and Cox have been under surveillance since the boy was abducted.'

'That'd be no problem. Someone like Tony Cox keeps his laundry basket stuffed with undeclared income. Putting his hand on a huge cash sum would be easy without even stepping outside the house. They have a safe, I bet?' Rory frowned, juggling the options. 'You're going to their place now? Woolpack Farm?'

'Yes. There's no time to lose. A pity. I was

enjoying our little chat.'

'May I come with you?'

Hayes hesitated, focussing on Smyth with suspicion. The chances were Smyth was no innocent bystander in all this. On the other hand he was an expert at this game, knew the type of criminals involved. In or out? On balance it was safer to keep an eye on him.

'OK, you're on. But discreetly. This is a delicate manoeuvre, one false step and the kid will be in danger and we don't know where Cox is holed up or why.'

'He may already be dead,' Rory flatly observed.

Twenty-three

Waller heard the car drive up to Woolpack Farm and waited for Hayes on the doorstep, drawing him aside to query Rory's existence.

'It's Robert Smyth, sir. Starewska's son. He speaks Russian and knows Tony Cox. He knows about the background stuff. I think he could be useful.'

'I hope he bloody understands the knife-edge we're on here. I want no cock-ups, Hayes. Getting the boy back safe is the priority.'

'Absolutely, sir. What's the current state of play?'

'We're waiting for a phone call to tell Mrs Cox where to pick up the kid. It could be some time. Cox has gone off to settle the deal but refuses, point blank, to have any police involvement, says Alexei will die unless he plays it straight.'

'When was all this fixed up?'

'Search me.' Waller looked seriously worried. 'We've been tapping the phones and put the mobiles out of reach. The woman's playing it cool, let Cox race off in his sports car without so much as a goodbye kiss.'

'They had a row?'

'Must've done. Do you think it's on the level this deal the two of them say is on the table? He's been going crackers, a nervous wreck, which is understandable, but Mrs Cox is pretty relaxed, convinced the boy will be turned over to her when she gets the signal where to go.'

'She admits there *is* a pay-off?'

'Says bugger all, and he's kept his mouth shut. If this doesn't work out, Hayes, I shall have the devil's own job explaining to the commissioner why we let them take the initiative.'

'Actually, Cox *did* get a phone call before we cut out communication. Bellamy was here and said Cox looked terrible after taking a call in his study.'

'What?! I said all calls to be monitored!'

'This one slipped in before we set up the fences. Cox said it was a business call, nothing to do with the disappearance of the boy. I've been talking to Smyth about this car sales racket of his. A head office in Moscow and a branch in St Petersburg. Makes a mint. The interesting thing is Cox was caught fiddling and Smyth was sent out to put a stop to it. Starewska, who was the actual owner, gave Cox the boot, just before she was killed.'

'But Cox wasn't even in the country then, was he?'

'No, but a bloody fortune's tied up in these car showrooms and Cox could have put out a contract on Mrs Starewska before anyone confirmed his being sacked.'

'This guy Smyth inherits the whole bag of tricks?'

'Yes, and he knew about his mother's plan to get rid of Cox. Cox thought Smyth was just the messenger, an accountant. He only found out that Smyth is Starewska's son and the new owner of Star Motors after Musset croaked. It was a secret between mother and son. Starewska found Rory a very useful tool. But even after the old woman died, Cox must have been hoping Smyth would reinstate him, would not be interested in running the Russian business. Smyth's got no experience of the car trade and might have been persuaded to let Cox keep his job.'

'Cox is playing a funny game, but paying a couple of Russian heavies to kill his boss just to keep his job? Sounds a bit over the top to me, matey.'

Hayes ploughed on, ignoring Waller's gibe. 'And now you've lost Cox? There was no unmarked car on his tail?'

'Well, that was the deal. But I couldn't swallow it,' Waller admitted, glaring furiously at Hayes, daring him to question the wisdom of any double cross at such a precarious juncture.

'You sent Bellamy after him?'

'Told him to keep his distance, with Preston and that DC Rogers as a back-up behind so Cox doesn't get suspicious.'

'Where are they now?'

'Just leaving the A40.'

'London?'

'Doubling back and forth, all over the shop, as if he's guessed we've put a tail on him.'

'You can't blame the guy for trying to go solo, sir. His kid's been kidnapped. We'd better go inside, I need to keep an eye on Smyth.'

The sitting room was almost deserted, only a constable and a WPC in evidence, their untidy jump to attention as the superintendent and Hayes came in bringing a certain frisson back into play.

'Where's Mrs Cox?' Waller barked.

'In the barn, sir. DC Robbins is with her and the older man who arrived just now with the DCI. She said she had some work to do.'

Waller coloured up, his face darkening. 'What?'

'In the barn, sir, her workshop. That's all right, isn't it?'

'She said it would calm her nerves,' the WPC put in, a fresh-faced girl Hayes didn't remember seeing before.

Waller looked shagged out, the tension building in the atmosphere like a ticking time bomb.

Hayes quickly intervened. 'Why don't you buzz off and brew up some coffee for the superintendent, constable? I'll go over to the barn and see what Mrs Cox is up to.'

Waller sank on to the sofa, staring round at the bizarre decoration of the room with its brick-coloured walls and dramatic oil paintings. He felt knackered and out of his depth with these people, if the truth was known. And a fucking kidnapping? A ransom? A pick-up at a secret location yet to be disclosed? And the possibility of a Russian hit mob right here on his patch? Nobody deserved a bundle of trouble like that. Perhaps it was time he retired. He lay back on the cushions and shut his eyes, hoping to get some kip in before the phone went and the race to fetch the kid was on.

Hayes had never seen a studio like it. The winter sunlight had drained away leaving the early evening dark as night. But the long table at the centre of the room was brilliantly illuminated from a fierce overhead light augmented by an anglepoise focussed on the work in progress. The blinds were down and the two figures poring over the bench threw long shadows against the walls. It was almost like a surgical theatre, a syringe, a scalpel and tweezers laid out on the bench together with cotton wool and a pile of flannel squares, the patient being a painting on a wooden panel, the image almost entirely obscured by dirt and a bitumen-like veneer.

Smyth looked up, smiling, greeting Hayes with a wordless salute. Tessa Cox continued working, her concentration complete. In the shadows Jenny Robbins stood sentinel by the phone on the desk. Hayes moved forward to stand behind Tessa, who continued, immersed in her task.

'What's going on?' Hayes amiably enquired.

'This is absolutely fascinating, Hayes. Tessa's doing a magical transformation before our very eyes.'

She looked up at this, a slight smile lifting

one corner of her mouth. 'It keeps me sane while I'm waiting for the phone to ring. It's not magic, more like spring cleaning. I'll explain as I go along, shall I?

'This is an old icon. We can judge the period by the age of the wood and the thickness of the panel. When cleats are used to join two sections, one gets more clues. On the old panels the painted area is hollowed out, leaving a bevelled edge – like here.' She ran a finger over the outer rim and the two men bent under the spotlight to get a closer look.

'And you cleaned icons like this for Mrs Starewska?'

'Oh yes. Amazing work. New to me at first but Lulu gave me a lot of guidance.' She put on rubber gloves and started brushing the panel with a pad of cotton wool. 'Ordinary sunflower oil,' she said, 'just to wipe off the surface dirt.' She then dipped a square of flannel into an evil-smelling liquid and lay it on a section of the painting, which she then covered with a pane of clear glass held down under a weight.

'What are these holes? Damage? Mr Musset explained to me that after the Revolution icons were destroyed or broken up, even used to shore up gaps in a pig's sty.'

'Thousands were lost but an extraordinary

number saved. Religion went underground but could not be entirely buried,' Tessa said solemnly. 'The holes you asked about are, in this case, where the metal overlay was nailed in place. A sort of frame with apertures disclosing the important parts of the work. Lulu's customers didn't care for the overlays. My job was often to remove the metal part and reveal the whole picture. I start with a completely black piece of wood, like you see here, and, hey presto, after just five minutes we have a peek as if through a keyhole at the glory underneath the veneer.'

Beads of oil had appeared on the underside of the glass. Tessa gently peeled off the flannel, revealing the dark surface now loosened, absorbed by the solvent. A wad soaked in more solvent was carefully wiped over the loosened varnish and Tessa used a scalpel to scrape off the bits still adhering to the surface. Then, like a coloured slide, a tiny section of a brilliant image was revealed. Smyth breathed a sigh of admiration and Hayes had to admit that a conjuring trick like that would be a hard act to follow.

'And this is an early work?' Smyth whispered.

'Probably not. That's the intriguing thing about this type of restoration. People would not waste a nice panel like this so, once the painting got discoloured, the image would be over-painted and then re-varnished. There could be several layers piled up one on top of the other like a plate of pancakes. I could remove all this top painting in the wild hope that eventually I'd hit the original fifteenth-century icon to comply with the estimated age of the panel.'

'You'd scrub away, trusting in your own intuition?'

She laughed. 'There's a certain experience comes into play, too, but yes, I could "scrub away" as you put it, inspector, and destroy the whole thing. It happens. But, if I'm right, the bedrock is the layer that's really valuable. Most of the very earliest works, eleventh and twelfth, even tenth century, are in museums but it's astonishing how many Byzantine icons appear at auction and with over thirteen thousand stored in the Hermitage it's not surprising there's a flourishing black market, especially among these new oil billionaires who get hooked on a desire to build their own collections, a stake in their heritage once the novelty of new houses and new cars wears off.'

'There are fakes, of course,' Smyth insisted. 'Lulu had a sixth sense, could smell out a fake from fifty paces. And the ministry dealing with illegal exports listed thousands of genuine icons smuggled out worth billions of roubles. At the end of the twentieth century, in one year alone, thirty icon dealers were shot either by the KGB or the mafia. Do you wonder that I have no desire to continue trading from a resurrected Star Gallery?'

'I had no idea so much money was involved,' Hayes murmured.

'It's not just icons,' Tessa countered. 'Fakes are features of all aspects of the dark side of the art market. The danger starts when the nouveau set is willing to employ criminals to achieve its ends.'

The phone rang and Robbins spun round to pull Tessa over to answer it. The message was brief and she merely repeated the location, her voice barely a whisper. 'The Cater Club sports ground just outside Marlow. Midnight. Got it. I'll be there.'

Twenty-four

Sergeant Bellamy kept his distance behind Cox's sports car, his own anonymous Toyota having no problem keeping at a safe distance, Cox's meandering route increasingly puzzling.

After leaving the A40 Cox slipped off into a side road and Bellamy was obliged to drop back and let the second police car take up the running. The night was dark, dense clouds obscuring the moon, the sparsely populated villages through which they passed rarely lit. Two hours passed in a seemingly cat and mouse charade, and Bellamy grew increasingly worried. He phoned Hayes on his mobile and described the roundabout route, if it was indeed a route, they were following.

'Do you think he's leading us a dance, sir, or just hoping to shake us off? We've been bloody careful, if he *has* spotted a tail I'd be surprised. Preston's up front now in a Range Rover in case we have to cut across country if Cox has a second vehicle lined up somewhere along the way.'

'Has Cox got a car phone?'

'Yes. Buller gave all the Cox vehicles a quiet dekko while we were hanging about the farm this afternoon but Cox didn't use the Mercedes before tonight so he's not had a chance of any secret negotiations before he set off.'

'And you've no idea where he's going? He must have covered a hundred and fifty miles at least and—'

'Sorry, sir, got to go. Preston's pulling a right. We're heading towards Milton Keynes.'

'He's making for the M1?'

'Seems like it.'

'Well, don't lose him, Bellamy, that hot rod of his could leave you standing.'

Bellamy shot off to catch up with Preston and after twenty minutes they joined the motorway. Shadowing Cox's Mercedes was easier in the heavy traffic and, with a speed restriction, he would not chance attracting a traffic cop's attention. Cox pulled into a motorway service station to fill up with petrol, and Bellamy followed suit, pulling a baseball cap low over his forehead and giving a discreet signal to Preston to stay in the Rover ready for a swift take-off if Cox made a fast getaway.

In fact, their quarry pulled over to a parking space and sauntered into the cafeteria for a bite to eat. He moved stiffly, a man pole-axed from lack of sleep and a long, tense drive. Bellamy cornered DC Rogers and told him to stay with the target while he went for a rain-check with Preston. He dropped into the passenger seat and pulled a map from under the dashboard, tracing their circuitous route with a biro.

'What d'you reckon he's up to, Mike?'

'Blowed if I know. There's no sense in it unless he's just filling in time. This drop zone must've been fixed yesterday. He's had no chance of getting a tip-off since we moved in and his wife's been nowhere.'

'Though he could have got directions by car phone after leaving. Or the two of 'em cooked up a plan last night. If the kid wasn't involved I'd run him in if I was Waller, there's something fishy going on. Perhaps we're being dragged off-course so the wife can pull a fast one. We've only got their word for it about doing the drop first and waiting till it's confirmed before giving the woman the OK to rendezvous and pick up the kid.'

Bellamy's mobile shrilled.

'Yeah? Right, I'll follow him through and

Mike'll stay here and cover the exit.'

Bellamy turned to Preston. 'That was Rogers. Cox has gone for a leak. I bet this is the pay-off point, Mike.' He leapt out and ran into the foyer, disappearing into the brightly lit entrance to follow Cox into the gents. Rogers was already standing at a urinal, making an impressive go of it. He winked at Bellamy and indicated the closed door of a cubicle as he washed his hands. A man came in to use the facilities, his shifty glance swiftly averted before immediately scuttling out. Did they so obviously look like cops, Bellamy wondered.

He buried his face in a paper towel as the cubicle door swung open and Cox crossed to the hand basins. Bellamy walked out and Rogers, a face unknown to their target, nodded companionably before following him, leaving Cox to finish up. Bellamy and Rogers split up, Bellamy immersing himself in a rack of postcards and the younger man lighting a cigarette and watching the area on a CCTV monitor behind the news-stand counter.

Cox looked terrible, his eyes baggy, his smooth suit creased and his shirt stained with what Bellamy guessed from the unsteadiness of his gait to be whisky. He prayed that no eagle-eyed patrolman would pull over their man for a breath test and foul up the whole operation. Cox glanced around then made a sudden bolt for it, making a shambling trot back to his car.

Bellamy grabbed Rogers. 'Close up the fucking gents and take the place apart. He's left the drop in the cubicle, inside the cistern or somewhere. I'll follow Preston and pull Cox in as soon as you ring me and confirm you've got the bag. Did he take anything in with him? A package? Leave anything in the tash can?'

Rogers emphatically shook his head and made back to the toilet block as Bellamy streaked off.

Cox was slow getting away and Preston was already idling at the junction by the time the Mercedes pulled out. Bellamy slipped in close behind, no longer fearful of being spotted, certain Cox's crafty move to leave the ransom in a prearranged cubicle at a prearranged time was the answer.

Their target shot off at speed once he reached the exit, moving into the fast lane towards Luton. Towards the bloody airport, Bellamy fumed. He needed back-up. At the first opportunity he'd get Hayes to set up something to keep Cox in the country at least until the kid was safely under wraps. Bellamy overtook Preston and surged ahead, forcing his engine to match the souped-up vehicle. But at junction eleven Cox peeled off and drew Bellamy and his mate into a tangle of B roads, breaking away north and heading out towards open countryside. It started to rain, a soft drizzle that misted the windscreen and fogged Bellamy's exhausted gaze as he accelerated into the darkness behind the glinting rear lights.

And then, without so much as a brake light warning, there was an almighty bang up ahead and a ball of flame lit up the wooded lane. Bellamy's wheels slowed to a halt as he braked just in time. The carnage was absolute. Cox's beautiful motor was engulfed in flames, the exploding fuel tank lighting up the December sky like a beacon. Bellamy climbed out of the car, aware that there was nothing he could do. Preston drew alongside, already phoning for the emergency services.

Bellamy was almost speechless with shock but, as Preston joined him to watch the conflagration, he muttered, 'What made him do that, Mike? To swerve straight into a brick wall to hit it head on? Suicide, d'you think?'

Preston shrugged. 'He was pissed, of course. Even so ... By the way, Roy, I checked with Rogers; the toilets were clean as a whistle, no drop. He checked all the cubicles, even the broom cupboard in case Cox slipped something in before we got there.'

'Cox never dumped any fucking ransom?'

'Nope.'

'Well, that puts the lid on it. No cash, no kid. Who's going to tell Waller?'

'I'll speak to the DCI, see what he can do to square it with the emergency services. We don't want them to think we chased the poor bugger into a brick wall, do we?'

Bellamy sighed and walked away, surveying the burning vehicle from the other side of the road. A man ran out from the gates of what Bellamy guessed must be a school, the crash site causing him to fall back in dismay, shielding his face from the heat of the blaze.

Bellamy drew the man away and pulled out his ID card. 'We're police officers, sir. Help is on the way.'

'Too late for this poor devil,' he replied. 'Thank God the boys have gone back for the holidays. You will have to clear this up, it's blocking the road. These sports car maniacs have got no sense; it's not even a black spot, officer, not even on a bend, I can't understand it.'

'A wet night?' Bellamy suggested. He pushed the man away from the fire, leaving Preston to calm down their inconvenient witness. But Preston left the man to stand in the road, hurrying towards Bellamy, his mobile clutched in his hand.

'I've just passed on the news to Hayes about no pay-out. I said Cox must have had the cash in the car all the time, hadn't even got to the drop before he crashed. But what d'you reckon, Roy? Cox's wife's ready to leave. Got the go-ahead to pick up the boy from Marlow at midnight. Hayes can't make it out. If Cox didn't pay up why was she given the all-clear? You sure we didn't miss something, Roy? I told Rogers to wait at the service station. Christ knows what Waller's going to say.'

'Is Hayes going with Mrs Cox?'

'He's gone on ahead to be hidden at the rendezvous before she arrives. Robbins is going to be crouched down in the back behind her and that's as far as Mrs Cox is prepared to go. But Hayes is never going to leave it at that, is he?'

Bellamy looked distinctly rattled. 'It's a right bloody buggers' muddle. I can't see the logic of it, Mike. We go on this wild goose chase after Cox and all the time there's no bleeding ransom at all unless it went up in smoke with his car. What were they playing at? Is Hayes going to break the bad news to the wife?'

'I doubt it. There's enough complications without telling her "Hubby's just driven into a brick wall, missus." Let's hope his alcohol count lets us off the hook. We *were* up his backside, no question, and he was driving like a man on the run, eighty miles an hour at the least and us no more than a hundred yards behind.'

Twenty-five

Hayes drove to the sports ground outside Marlow with an hour to spare, determined to be in place before Tessa Cox arrived to collect Alexei at midnight. Smyth was hanging in there, insisting on being at the rendezvous with Hayes. Waller was set against allowing Smyth so close to the action but, as a man who was familiar with Cox and his dubious business dealings, the superintendent decided to let Hayes handle it while he tried to sort out the debacle of Cox's apparent suicide. It was vital to exonerate Bellamy and the other lads from any charge of police harassment, and he instructed his driver to bring the flashing lights and sirens into play for a dash up the M1 to attend the crash site.

Hayes pulled his vehicle into a belt of trees behind the cricket pavilion of the deserted Cator Sports Club and cut the lights. Smyth sat tight in the passenger seat, making his presence as polite as the situation allowed.

Two police cars had followed at a discreet distance and were under strict orders to stay out of sight off the approach road but within close proximity to the pavilion.

'You think the kid will be brought here for a pick-up at the pavilion?' Rory whispered.

'Seems logical. Not that any of this seems logical. If Cox was meant to pass over the ransom before his wife was informed of the time and venue we've missed something. Bellamy swears they've been watching his every move but there's no sense in it if nothing's been handed over in exchange for the boy.'

'Unless Cox promised to pay up when he got back to Moscow?'

Hayes laughed bitterly. 'From my experience, no villain would accept an IOU, especially with criminal charges in the offing.'

Rory sighed. 'Yes, you're right. I wouldn't trust Cox an inch even with his boy in danger, but once Alexei's free the chances of a settlement would be blown away completely. A dangerous game, though, you've no idea how long a mafia vendetta can be held over a man's head, Hayes. These people have suffered from decades of summary executions, a bullet through the head's the kindest way to go. My poor mother was battered to a pulp.'

They shared a flask of coffee and passed the time reminiscing about their years in Oxford.

'I went back to live there after I got out of prison.'

'Yeah, the fraud. I heard you'd done time.'

'I was just a kid, stupid as they come, but Oxford was the nearest to any sort of home ground once the Smyths had written me off. I don't blame them, I was a big disappointment.'

'What was the scam?'

'Fiddling student funds for a start, then embezzling my employers, a vacation job with a firm of solicitors. Not a hell of a lot of money in it, certainly not worth doing time for, but I thought I was fireproof. After that Lulu took me in hand and I've been clean ever since. I owe her everything,' he murmured.

Hayes made a quiet call to the other cars and reiterated the necessity to keep hidden. 'As soon as you spot an approaching vehicle entering the club gates, be ready to close all exits. But not, I repeat not, until I give the signal. Mrs Cox will be driving a Jeep so let her through. She doesn't know she's got police company.'

'You told her only Jenny Robbins was in

attendance?'

'Sure. No way Tessa Cox was going to agree to a posse. We just have to keep our heads down until the boy's safely back in the Jeep.'

'You should have organized an armed response.'

'Waller got cold feet, scared shitless at the prospect of a shoot-out with a kid involved.'

Rory sighed, wondering if all police reactions were as haphazard as this.

Time ticked by, the empty field now shrouded in a thick mist, Hayes' restricted view of the approach road further impaired by drenching rain. At last the headlights of the Jeep appeared through the gates and Tessa pulled on to the grass and reversed to back on to the pavilion. She doused the lights and the sound of the car engine petered out, leaving the place unnervingly silent.

Tessa climbed out and leant against the bonnet to light a cigarette. The burning tip gleamed in the darkness as the minutes ticked by, her calm, as they all waited, a miracle of composure. She threw away the stub and reached inside the Jeep to pull out a slim leather case. An art folder? It was difficult to make out in the gloom. Hayes' thoughts surged at the sudden realization that *here* was the bloody ransom money, not

211

with Cox at all! Tessa had had control of the pay-off all the time.

But this was not the moment to call her bluff and blow the operation sky high. The important thing was to see the boy safe first. Thank God he had the hidden police back-up ready to zoom in as soon as the exchange was under wraps. That was the snag with kidnapping; picking up the ransom was the dangerous bit.

Hayes kept his concerns to himself and Rory, from his blinkered view of the scene hunkered down in the passenger seat, seemed oblivious of Tessa's sleight of hand with the ransom, if that was what it was.

The sports club was clearly an expensive leisure facility for the moneyed population living on the outskirts of a fashionable river-side locale. Beyond the cricket pitch and pavilion several tennis courts lay under a foggy blanket, only a single security light blinking like a red eye above the porch of what Hayes presumed to be a shower block. The pavilion was a handsome building, large enough for social evenings and with an extensive parking area to the rear. Far away a church clock chimed the half-hour.

Hayes glanced at his watch, clearly baffled by the absence of any movement from either the Jeep or any vehicle approaching the gates.

'Do you think Cox scuppered the deal before the crash?' Rory suggested.

'Christ knows. You knew the guy. Surely he wouldn't gamble with his kid's life?'

'He could have changed the venue, agreed to pick up Alexei himself. Sounds OK to me. The man with the ransom exchanges it directly for the boy. Trouble was he hit a brick wall on the way.'

'You think it was an accident?'

Rory paused, deep in thought. 'You've got to understand the situation. Cox was running a smuggling ring, probably with Dmitri, Lulu's agent, though we don't know if it was Dmitri for sure and chances are we'll never see him again after all this, especially with both Lulu and Musset dead. Cox was in an excellent position to bring stuff in and out hidden in his luxury cars, welded under the chassis or wherever. When I was given the job of blowing him off, Cox must have still had one – or even more than one –big deal in the pipeline and it was too late to call it off. Abducting his kid was a sure way to focus the bloke's attention if Cox can, in fact, see it through. If he hasn't got the merchandise Cox is in a bear trap. Lulu's given him the push so he's lost his job, and running back to England without completing the deal won't save him. They never give up, these thugs. If Cox couldn't settle up, he was dead meat.'

'He killed himself?'

Rory's reply was drowned in the roar of a helicopter circling overhead and in a blinding revelation Hayes knew he had miscalculated. Tessa's Jeep surged forward as the helicopter settled down on the field and within seconds the door was open and two men jumped down to join her, the blades still circulating in an ear-splitting rhythm.

'Jesus! We're going to miss it!' Hayes shouted, scrambling from the car with Rory at his heels as they raced out of the trees to grapple with the two men. Tessa was thrown to the ground in the mêlée, Jenny snatching the portfolio from Tessa's grasp as they wrestled for it, a woman's screams shrilling from the open door of the helicopter adding to the cacophony.

Hayes pinned one of the men by the throat and they fought in the darkness, rolling over and over on the sodden turf. Rory made a running tackle at the slighter one of the two but the man slipped from his grasp like an eel, retrieving the portfolio from where it had fallen as the women continued to fling punches at each other, and reached the helicopter just as the hysterical woman pulled him inside. She clung to the hatch and stood yelling incomprehensibly within the lighted doorway. As the helicopter started to rise she turned back to toss out what looked like a bundle of bedding before being hurled back inside as the door closed. The machine rose in the air with a deafening roar as the police cars, with flashing lights and sirens, slew onto the field too late to pick up the pieces.

Hayes clung on to his captive, his eyes venomous. Rory rose painfully to his feet to see Tessa running towards the ditched cargo, Jenny lying unconscious in the mud. A wail issued from the bundled duvet as she flung herself on to it.

'It's the kid!' Hayes roared. 'She's got the kid.'

He ran to her side and, between them, they untrussed the small body. Tessa smiled and wiped a streak of blood from her face. 'It's all right, kiddo,' she said with a shaky grin. 'You're home now.'

Twenty-six

Hayes detailed the police contingent to take charge of their captive before limping over to check on Jenny Robbins, who was starting to come round.

He bent down. 'You OK, Robbins?'

She scowled. 'Bloody silly question. I did something to my shoulder when I fell. That woman's got a kick like a mule, you'd never guess we were supposed to be on the same side.'

Rory joined them and helped her to sit up. 'Tessa was intent on keeping hold of the bag.'

'The skinny bloke got away with it,' Hayes admitted. 'Bad luck there.'

Rory looked thoughtful. 'We'll see. I'd like to be in on the interview with the Russian, if that's all right with you.'

'That'd be Waller's decision, but he *is* Russian?'

'From the foul-mouthed expletives thrown at me, born and bred, no question.'

'I've told my lads to whisk him back to Renham before any questions are asked. He *was* detained in the course of a planned operation so Waller should be able to swing it.' He leant over to reassure Jenny. 'I've called an ambulance, Robbins. It should be here soon.'

She struggled in an attempt to stand but fell back in agony. 'I'm sure it's just a sprain, sir, no need for hospital.'

'Sorry, but best be sure. Anyway, I want the kid checked over, he may have been injured when he was shoved from the helicopter. I had a quick look and he seems OK but he's only wearing pyjamas so being wrapped in the duvet was brilliant. I suggested Tessa Cox and Alexei be kept in overnight.'

At that moment an ambulance drove through the gates and bumped over the grass to where Tessa sat hugging the boy and laughing. Alexei had quickly recovered from the terror of being tossed from the helicopter and was now starting to enjoy the excitement. He was still bundled up in the duvet but became alarmed at the prospect of being shunted into an ambulance. He clung to Tessa, who struggled to her feet, urgently whispering into his ear as the burly ambulance man approached. 'It's just for a check-up, sweetie, I'll stay with you and as soon as we've found some warm clothes for you, we can go home. OK?'

Hayes hurried over and spoke to the driver, pointing to the second casualty now propped against the car, Rory engrossed in lighting a cigarette for her, doing the thing he was best at; being charming. Jenny was clearly in pain and nursed her arm as she drew on the cigarette, managing a tremulous laugh at something he was saying.

Hayes joined them. 'The ambulance will drive over here as soon as Cox and the boy are on board. I'll have to leave you, Robbins, Waller's been on the phone and wants me back straight away. I've asked the WPC here to travel in the ambulance with you.'

'In case Tessa throws another right hook?' Jenny jeered. 'What's her game, sir? Whose side is she on?'

He shrugged. 'It's too complicated to explain now but I want to get her to the station in the morning to answer some questions.'

'Well, I hope she's not going to walk away from this scot-free, sir.'

'Did she make any calls from the car after you both left the farm?'

'No, hardly spoke, clearly had it all worked out, though. While we were waiting for the pick-up, she grabbed the portfolio from the foot well at the front. It must have been hidden under a blanket or something, I didn't see her put anything in the boot when we left. I wasn't even sure we would be using the Jeep till the last minute.'

'An uncomfortable journey for you,' Rory said.

'Terrible. I couldn't see out and madam up front wasn't being sociable; we didn't guess there were police cars hidden round the field, though. I got quite jittery when we stopped and she started rummaging in the foot well. Could have brought out a bloody shotgun to finish me off, for all I knew.'

The ambulance trundled alongside and, after close questioning their patient, lifted Jenny into a wheelchair and put her inside with Tessa and Alexei. A WPC was insisting on travelling with them and Jenny managed a weak smile as the doors slammed shut.

'You didn't tell Jenny about Tony Cox's accident,' Rory said.

'Best keep it under wraps till we get Mrs Cox back on home ground. Waller will want to throw in a shock factor before we interview her.'

'Sounds brutal.'

'Yeah, well, we have to use every advantage, aim below the belt if necessary. I nicked a sample of her cleaning fluid before I left the barn after that astonishing demonstration on the icon. You seen anything like that before, Rory?'

'No. But I've seen these treasures in their original state often enough. Nobody cared a tinker's cuss about all that religious tat when the churches were dismantled. The valuable stuff was put under lock and key in museums but thousands of icons were put in store and once the word got out that money could be made in the West, the black market moved in and stacks just disappeared, rubbish and fakes included. The legitimate sales involve agents scouring the countryside for those icons that had been hidden away and they are mostly in such poor condition even expensive reclamation is out of the question. Tessa's one of the few British experts in icon repair but there are dozens in Europe and many even more experienced restorers working for the museums in Moscow and St Petersburg.'

Rory frowned and withdrew into a silent reverie. Hayes made a quick phone call back to base and when the call was concluded Smyth was studying a flight timetable and making pencilled notes in his diary. Clearly, Hayes ironically conjectured, a busy man, a guy with no more time to share on this exciting break in his business schedule.

Next morning Tessa Cox was allowed to drive home with the boy. One of the volunteers working in the children's ward had kindly offered to go out and buy trainers and a tracksuit for Alexei. He seemed none the worse for his adventure, though refusing to say a word about Vera, his mother.

Jenny was forcibly detained for a pep talk from the physio.

'It's only a broken collar bone,' she complained to the junior doctor on duty in Accident & Emergency. 'I could go home.'

'How?' he countered, his face lighting up. 'You can't drive and your boss said to keep you here until he sent someone.'

'Brilliant!' she muttered. 'What happened to the lady and her son who were brought in with me last night? Mrs Cox.'

'No idea. Probably discharged herself. The child wasn't injured. We're putting you in a ward for the present, the therapist wants a word before you go.'

Jenny found herself in a crowded ward with several ambulant patients and a harassed nursing staff. At least one of the elderly women was mentally infirm and had continually to be led back to her chair in front of the television.

When Mark Morrison appeared following a particularly nasty lunch on a tray, Jenny could have hugged him to death except that her shoulder felt like an elephant had stamped on it.

'Mark! You angel. Who told you I was here?'

'Hayes. I phoned the station and they said you'd been injured on special duty. I imagined gunshot wounds at the very least but I gather you were in a fist fight.'

'With a bloody black belt. Your ex-girlfriend, Tessa Cox, uses her feet. She connected with my head and I broke a collarbone when I went down and knocked myself out.'

He laughed. 'And that's it?'

'It's not funny,' she fumed, edging him away from the curious glances of the other visitors. 'Did Hayes say I could leave?'

Mark nodded. 'Why else would I take two weeks off? I'm driving you. Hayes doesn't want you back till the doc says you're fit for work. How about a nice convalescence in Cornwall? My parents have a cottage on the coast. Not exactly St Tropez and with wild weather we might be holed up over Christmas. Are you on?'

It took Jenny all of five seconds to discharge herself into the care of this entirely unforeseen knight in shining armour.

Outside in the car he spelt out the whole deal. 'My sister's about your size. She leaves her sailing gear at the cottage all year. Plenty of jumpers and I've packed a bag for myself. We can stop on the way down so you can buy what else you think you'll need, OK?'

She had never been taken over in such style before and decided she liked it. She stole a glance at Mark Morrison's set jaw as he manoeuvred out of the car park and concluded life was just too damned unpredictable.

She felt light-headed; the painkillers she guessed. Just when she had been felled by a body blow, abandoned – even the WPC hadn't come in to bid her goodbye – a man she hardly knew turns up and takes control. Jenny decided not to mention that with her arm in a sling he'd be doing all the washing up. And as for the cooking, well, she was rubbish in the kitchen department even without the excuse of a broken collar bone.

Twenty-seven

Next morning Hayes reported to Waller on the dot of nine, finding the big fella back in his own familiar surroundings at the station and clearly in a celebratory mood.

Waller rubbed his hands. 'Great work, Hayes. Take a seat.'

Hayes dropped into a chair and nodded, his mood tense. He had slept badly, the drama of the rescue playing over and over in his brain, but snagging at the same point, like a scratched record.

Waller launched into an enthusiastic tactical plan, impervious to Hayes' muted response. He remained adamant that Tessa Cox had a lot to answer for and was in the process of applying for a search warrant for the farm. It had been agreed that she be brought in for questioning after Hayes had broken the news about her husband's accident. Smyth was to be allowed in the viewing room while the Russian – whose name, it was discovered, was Sergei Popov – was interviewed.

'An official interpreter has been secured from the Russian embassy and a British lawyer appointed for his defence,' Waller continued, 'but the questioning of Popov is to be delayed pending the forensic examination of a knife found strapped to his ankle.'

Hayes stiffened. 'I'm not sure we haven't been too easy with Smyth, sir. He's wangled his way into the investigation and I admit I've let him have more rope than anyone on the outside would normally have. But this request of his to be in on the Popov interview? Has the commissioner OK'd it?'

Waller tossed these remarks aside with an irritable shrug. 'Can we *trust* these Ruskie interpreters, Hayes? If their man from the embassy tells me one thing, how am I to know if it's kosher? He could translate it any way suits them and we'd be none the wiser. Popov's only being questioned on an assault on Darren Porter so far. We can hardly justify the expense of a *second* bloody interpreter! Be practical, Hayes. If Smyth's willing to vouch for the official version that's good enough for me, no need to drag the Commissioner into it or we'll be stepping into a pile of shit, not to mention my budget. You got doubts about Smyth, Hayes?'

'Well, he has got form, sir.'

'Years ago, mate! He's a respectable business man now, isn't he? Anyway, he's only looking on from the viewing room, not authorized to be in on the interview. And if the stakes get any higher and we can hook this Popov into the Starewska murder then we can splash out on an independent interpreter.'

'What about Popov's role in the kidnapping?'

Waller was obviously seriously losing it with Hayes' pussyfooting around, and he rose from his chair in a clear indication that the discussion was at an end. Hayes scrambled to his feet.

'You amaze me, Hayes. You bring Smyth in from the cold, treat him like a white man, then start iffing and butting when he volunteers his services as a specialist who not only speaks the lingo like a native but knows the methods these Russian mafia gangs use. He's not costing us anything, is he? And as it's his own mother who was killed by these thugs; he's hardly biased in their favour, is he?'

'Well, no, of course not. But I said I'd confirm whether we would need him to be on hand for Popov's interview. If the commissioner's happy, I'll give him a ring, shall I?'

'That's what I said, didn't you hear me first time, chief inspector?'

Waller's manner was now dangerously heated and Hayes quickly apologized and turned to go, closing the door quietly behind him.

Hayes arrived at the farm to find Alexei decorating the Christmas tree in the hall. A woman in an overall appeared from the dining room, trailing a vacuum cleaner. The boy looked up and smiled, his eyes bright as any nine-year-old's at the prospect of Christmas.

'Madam's in the barn,' she said in a thick accent, ruffling the boy's hair as she passed. 'I call her for you?'

'No, I know where to find her.'

The atmosphere in the house was relaxed, no hint of the emotional turmoil occasioned by the kidnap. Alexei was entirely at ease, the adventure already shelved, Hayes hoped, in a comfort zone established by the affectionate routine of the Cox household. Such resilience in the young was astonishing but perhaps, to a child, the reality of such an extraordinary weekend was no more relevant than a computer game with its cops and robbers, bad guys and airborne rescues.

Outside, he made a quick phone call to Rory, who answered with the mumbled response of a man dredged from the bottom of the sea.

'Hey, Rory! Sorry, did I wake you? Still recovering from two rounds with a Russian mobster?'

'Yeah, well, I'm not as fit as I was. Terrific fun, though. I'll be dining out on it for years. What's the latest?'

'An embassy interpreter is being sent down to cover the interview after the forensic guys have examined the knife Popov was carrying. They're hoping to get evidence connecting him to your mother's murder but, in the meantime, there's nothing likely to stick on the charge sheet except beating up a kid called Porter.'

Rory blew out his cheeks in dismay. One lucky punch only just saving Hayes from a possible stabbing? 'Do you realize I'm sixty years of age, Hayes? Got my free bus pass only last week and I nearly KO a professional hit man. Amazing!'

Hayes laughed. 'An unequal bout. But let's face it, Rory, you let him get away, he escaped to the helicopter with the bloody ransom!' There was no answer to that and Hayes frowned at the recollection. 'I'll call you back as soon as Waller fixes up the Popov interview, shall I? If you're still interested, that is.'

Rory mumbled his assent and broke off,

back to Dreamland, Hayes guessed. Being a dilettante sounded great, no nine to five for Robert Smyth, the jammy blighter.

He knocked on the barn door and found Tessa filling a cardboard packing case. She looked up, her eyes wary. 'I must thank you, chief inspector, for saving Alexei.'

'He seems OK.'

'Kids are enormously resilient. By the time he goes back to school after Christmas he will have relegated the whole episode to second place after his skiing holiday.'

'Are you certain? Being with his mother was important, I'm sure. Has he asked about her?'

'Not a word. What will happen to Vera? We don't want to press charges, no harm was done.'

'It's not as simple as that. As it happens Vera Cox seems to have disappeared.'

'Gone back to Russia, I imagine.'

'How?'

'She must have hitched a ride to Paris or Ireland on the helicopter.'

Light dawned. 'She was the woman who pushed Alexei out?'

'Yes, I'm sure of it. I only caught a glimpse but who else would put the boy's welfare first? If she hadn't pushed him out he would have been whisked away to God knows where. She loves him, Hayes. When Alexei feels able to talk about it I can explain it to him. Perhaps, in the course of time, he will be able to see her again.'

'Not in the UK, Mrs Cox. Vera abducted the boy and set in motion a police hunt costing a great deal of money. The courts take a dim view.'

'She was persuaded by those men. Vera could never have organized the snatch herself. These people have made her believe it would be nothing more than a home visit, I expect, and as she had been in touch with Alexei by phone he would have told her about his exciting school trip to France. It was his first holiday without Tony or myself, it was the sort of thing a child would boast about, his first taste of independence. Do you know where she took him?'

'No. I was hoping you would know. One of the men arrested will be questioned later. We hope to get details of the plan eventually. At present we are more interested in the murder investigation now that Alexei is home.'

Tessa finished taping up the box and sat at the table, her exhausted gaze sliding round the room now bright with winter sunshine, the polished equipment glinting on the bench as if in readiness for an autopsy.

'I'm expecting Tony to call. I tried to ring him several times last night from the hospital to give him the good news that Alexei was safe but his mobile was off. I can't think what he's playing at,' she added crossly.

'I've some bad news, I'm afraid. We delayed informing you until Alexei was home but there was an accident last night.'

She stiffened, her eyes wide with fear. 'Not Tony?'

'I'm afraid so. His car crashed into a wall and burst into flames. Death was instantaneous. I am so sorry.'

Her hands flew to her mouth, and, visibly shaking, she focussed on Hayes like a rabbit caught in a trap.

Hayes was never the right man to break bad news, his words, however much he attempted to phrase them, coming across harshly. 'Can I get you a drink, Mrs Cox? Would you like to go back to the house?'

She shook her head and, after a moment, crossed to the sink to fill a beaker from the tap. She sipped the water, her eyes averted, but finally put the glass aside and faced him, her composure hardening. Hayes' mind flew back to that other occasion when he had witnessed Tessa Cox's distress, in Dolly Froude's cottage after she had discovered Starewska's body. It had to be admitted the woman had guts.

'Was it suicide?'

'I think so. There will be an inquest, of course.' He hesitated for a split second. 'There are witnesses. Your husband was being followed, Mrs Cox. We had reason to believe he was in a conspiracy regarding the kidnap.'

She shook her head in disbelief. 'Your men saw him crash the car?'

'It was an extraordinary accident, there seems to be no explanation. Perhaps you have some information to help us?'

She turned away, her shoulders set. 'No, I haven't. But I hope an accidental verdict is recorded for Alexei's sake. With both parents gone the poor child has only me.'

Hayes let the silence fill the room before placing the killer blow. 'I'm afraid I must ask you to accompany me to the station, Mrs Cox. There are a number of inconsistencies to be dealt with and unfortunately we are unable to delay the questioning. We need to apprehend Mrs Starewska's killer before anyone else dies.'

Tessa braced herself against the sink but when she answered her voice was firm. 'Yes, of course. I'll just get a coat and arrange with my housekeeper to stay with Alexei till I get back. This won't take long, will it, chief inspector? Obviously I have a lot to organize. Has Tony's body been recovered from the wreck?'

Waller took the chance to see his prisoner as he was led off to a cell. And it was quite an eyeful, the man's muscular arms tattooed with a fantastic variety of designs; crosses, incomprehensible Cyrillic script, flowers and chains. 'The man's a human comic strip, Buller. I've never seen anything like it. Any news about the knife?'

'Not yet, sir. But the DCI is hoping to tie it in with the old lady's murder.'

'Always the optimist!' Waller retorted, grinning like a gargoyle, tickled pink to be in control at last. The accident site had been cleared and Cox's body painstakingly transferred to the mortuary in Luton. The superintendent's negotiations with the local police had gone well despite the initial incomprehension of the complicated operation mounted to recover a missing boy whose alleged abduction was defiantly refuted by the child's stepmother, a woman who was herself under suspicion as a key witness in a murder enquiry.

But Waller's enthusiasm was unshakable and when he met Hayes escorting Tessa Cox to the interview room his cup overfloweth.

Twenty-eight

Tessa walked firmly into the interview room, head erect. She wore black jeans and a leather jacket, her pale face carefully made up, her mouth set.

Waller watched on the video link in the next room while Hayes and Bellamy conducted the interview. A WPC brought in mugs of tea and Hayes offered Tessa a cigarette, determined to keep the atmosphere as cool as possible. Tessa gave the strong tea a withering glance and refused the cigarette, glancing at the clock on the wall, the time creeping towards midday.

Hayes explained the procedure and after the initial formalities jumped in at the deep end.

'Shall we start with the discovery of Mrs Starewska's body?'

'I've gone over all that with your constable,' she snapped.

'Yes, of course,' Hayes patiently replied. 'But to clear the backlog of information I would like to return to the beginning. Tell me again. Why were you so anxious to call on the old lady on such a wet afternoon?'

'A question of work in progress. I wanted to consult Lulu before she went back to London that evening.'

'It was that urgent? So important that you were prepared to walk all of two miles to get her opinion? Opinion on what?'

'A technical problem. You wouldn't understand, Hayes.'

He sighed. 'You will have to bear with me, Mrs Cox, I'm a slow learner.'

She pinned him with an icy stare. 'Is this relevant? I had a problem and Lulu was conveniently close by for the weekend. Instead of wasting time chasing her back to London I decided to catch her before she drove back on Sunday night. I am impulsive, chief inspector, impatient, and, as my husband would say, single-minded when it comes to my work. Surely you can understand that?'

Bellamy broke in, treading carefully. 'We are trying to get everything in sequence, Mrs Cox. You brought nothing with you to Star Cottage? Nothing for Mrs Starewska to check? No equipment, solvents of any kind?'

'Nothing.'

'And you saw no one near the scene and

called the emergency services immediately?' Bellamy persisted, his dogged style calming the choppy waters.

In the viewing room Waller was becoming impatient, wishing now he had this saucy madam boxed in himself. That was the trouble with Hayes, he fumed, gets himself bamboozled by any pretty woman with a sharp line in back-chat.

'We shall move on, then, shall we?' Hayes said. 'Tell me about your husband's little sidelines. I apologize for being so unfeeling as to question you so soon after his death but we have to move on, Mrs Cox, and your testimony is vital.'

'What do you mean? His "little side-lines"?'

'We know that Mr Cox's car dealerships in Russia were financed by Mrs Starewska but I have it on good authority that he had, not to put too fine a point on it, been smuggling. He had been confronted by Mr Smyth and given a verbal dismissal by phone by Mrs Starewska. Tony had lost his job in effect. Did he tell you this?'

Tessa frowned. 'As a matter of fact, he did. Smyth was spreading lies about him and Lulu was taken in.'

'And that was the reason you were prepared to rush over to Bartram to try to

persuade Mrs Starewska to give him another chance?'

'No! How many times do I have to tell
you? I drove over to see Lulu on a technical
matter concerning the restoration of an
icon. Tony had mentioned that Lulu had
blasted him on the phone but he didn't take
it seriously. She had a quick temper and was
tricked by Smyth, a smooth operator who
wanted to seize control of the businesses in
Russia. He has, I gather, now succeeded.
Conned Lulu into changing her will.'

'Mr Smyth is her legitimate heir, her son,
in fact.'

'Bollocks! Did he tell you that?'

'The lawyer has verified it.'

Tessa slumped in her chair, her mind
fizzing.

Hayes pressed home his advantage. 'Your
husband came back here immediately after
the murder? You're sure of that? He wasn't
already in England when Mrs Starewska
died?'

'No! Of course he wasn't. I met him at the
airport. He came home to be with me and
we stayed at a hotel to talk things over.'

'But you're not sure, are you, Mrs Cox?
You don't know how deep was the trouble
he was in. He was a competent car salesman
and had had time to accumulate savings

from the Russian investment. Getting another job would have presented no problem, I'm sure, being thrown out of Star Motors was inconvenient but not so earth shattering as to cause him to drive into a brick wall, was it? Suicide, Mrs Cox, not an accident. He killed himself because he was in desperate trouble with his other scams, wasn't he? Smuggling, Mr Smyth insists. A greedy man, was he, Tony Cox? Seeing the mountain of roubles his clients had piled up made him envious? What were these little sidelines that got him involved in a game he couldn't win, Mrs Cox?'

She paled, visibly shaken, her startled response more than Hayes could hope for. 'Are you accusing me of being his accomplice?' she whispered.

'You're not under arrest. Yet. But yes, Mrs Cox, there are some unanswered questions hanging over you. Alexei's abduction was the last straw for Tony, wasn't it? Was the price too high? And if he couldn't stump up the ransom, who would? And if not, what would happen to his son and, worse still in his frantic state of mind, what would happen to him if Lulu Starewska's murder was any guide?'

Tessa leant on the table, her head in her hands, her dark hair obscuring her face. At last she looked up, her determination re-asserted, her strong will enfolding her like a flag.

'OK, Hayes. Tony's gone. Lulu's passed away. I'll tell you how it was. But I want a lawyer.'

Twenty-nine

It was late afternoon before Tessa and her lawyer were ready to resume the interview. Hayes grew increasingly anxious and checked and rechecked the pathologist's reports on Starewska's murder. Rory hung about the station, evidently trying to keep out of Waller's line of vision, Lulu's son being a debatable asset in a complicated line of enquiry. He invited Hayes to join him for lunch and in the limbo of waiting for the Russian interpreter to arrive and Tessa's lawyer to get his skates on, it seemed a good idea.

They repaired to the so-called gastropub in Renham, a tarted-up establishment, the main attraction being a dearth of pre-Christmas office lunches and, apart from a few sprigs of holly over the bar, a distinctly low-key yuletide atmosphere.

Hayes was beginning to worry about the approaching festivities. Pippa was campaigning for a family get-together in Swansea and Hayes was countering with a suggested week in the Austrian Alps. 'That's if the case is wrapped up by then,' he added. Pippa remained unimpressed but his reluctance to move into the cottage with her was unlikely to be mitigated by a jolly week-end with her family in Wales. He had been married before, of course, a bit of a disaster that predisposed him to caution.

Rory perked up after a double whisky and the menu looked promising. But they ordered liver and bacon to be on the safe side, the gastronomic wonders a dubious alternative. Hayes stuck with a half of lager and remained glum until the main course arrived and the background music muted.

'What do you think will come out of Popov's grilling, Hayes?'

'We've got the forensic evidence proving his knife is a fit for the stabbing but there's no blood linking it to Mrs Starewska's attack so we might have to string it along.'

'You mean kid him the evidence is there?'

'Not in so many words. Just infer that he's in the frame. What's your opinion, Rory?'

'Well, if he is one of these former camp guards indoctrinated from childhood to loyalty to the powers that be, he's going to be a hard nut to crack. These men have had a rough time in recent years, with little option but to join the mafia gangs or hitch up with a wealthy employer who needs protection. Has anyone seen him stripped to the waist? Do the tattoos conform to the designs I told you about?'

'No idea. Pity you lost the other guy who got away with the ransom money. Until we get Tessa Cox to explain it all, the organization of the pay-off stays a mystery. We don't know whether Tony was the bagman or not or how he and his wife concocted the plan. How much cash would you guess was involved, Rory? Cox was a wealthy man if he was dabbling in undercover deals in addition to his commission on sales. Will you keep the outlets in Moscow and St Petersburg? I know you're not convinced that reopening the gallery would be a good idea but have you decided anything yet?'

'Early days. I shall leave Ball to negotiate with the insurers about the gallery but I must fly out to Moscow as soon as possible to replace Cox. There is an assistant manager, a Russian, who knows the ropes and can run the show until I've checked the books. He's probably honest. From my knowledge of Cox he liked to keep all the pickings for himself. Only a fool would get involved in tax evasion and illegal cash transactions but money laundering via a legitimate business is rife. There is more than a handful of extremely wealthy Russians living in London and Paris. Men who hit the jackpot from the oil industry and manufacturing previously controlled by the Soviets, and such people sometimes have difficulty in spending all the dosh or getting it out of the country. I shall dispose of Lulu's gallery but keep the garages. It's a booming trade and as a Russian speaker I am familiar with the changing attitudes towards private enterprise. I also have a number of useful contacts in the government.'

'Well, your mother was Russian, wasn't she? Did she persuade you to learn the language?'

'She did. But her father was Polish, a political troublemaker living in St Petersburg, who married a local woman. When they were arrested Lulu fled to Paris. She found herself alone and moved to London and trained herself as an expert in Russian art. A fighter. A difficult woman, some would say, but with a background like that who could wonder?'

Hayes' mouth took a downturn; listening to a mature man banging on about his mother was not his forte. He pulled Rory back to the matter in hand. 'One of my men is trying to persuade our only witness, a young tearaway who claims to have seen two men take off in a motor boat the night of the murder, to come in. We're hoping to stage an identity parade, but it's proving difficult, the lad's allergic to the police. Buller is an exceptional officer with the right touch, and we need this kid's confirmation if only to nail Popov on an assault charge. He gave our boy a going-over when the two men realized they'd been spotted.'

Waller called Hayes into his office before the Cox interview began, Tessa and her lawyer already seated in the interview room.

'Now, don't pull any punches with this Cox woman, Hayes. She's as tricky as a sackload of monkeys. The brief's come down from London so don't throw anything at her we can't back up.'

Waller's ebullience remained undimmed, his self-assessment of his nifty handling of the Cox suicide as good as a Christmas box in his mind. Things were looking up and Buller had come up trumps with that little toerag Darren Porter. Persuaded him that 'As the suspect is "foreign" your mates'll be cheering that one of their gang is on the right side for once.' One of his pals even escorted Darren to the station, waving a St

244

George's flag, a leftover from the village supporters' party for the European Cup, and Darren strutted into the nick like a man selected for a medal.

As it turned out, it wasn't much of a show, Popov being picked out immediately.

'You sure, Darren? This is a murder enquiry, you know. You'll be asked about the assault if it comes to court.'

'No problem, Mr Buller. I won't let you down. And I got that job at the garage you put a word in for me with Mr Dudley about. My mum's over the moon. A new pair of overalls an'all, with Renham Motors printed on the back like I was on a pit stop team. Brill!'

Hayes walked into the interview room closely followed by Bellamy; Tessa Cox and her solicitor already seated.

'Shall we continue from where we left off this morning, Mrs Cox?'

Thirty

Tessa looked pale but composed, her solicitor, a young man who introduced himself as Peter Coman from Bliss, Goldman & Parker of Lincolns Inn, far less so. He placed a legal pad on the table and toyed with a gold biro, glancing anxiously from his client to Hayes and back to the blank sheet in front of him. Despite the legal eagle aura, Mr Coman, Hayes decided, had never been in a police interview room before, dealing only with respectable divorce cases perhaps. Luckily, Tessa Cox seemed well able to handle herself and, after the recording machine was set in motion, she started speaking, her voice firm, her account of the events leading up to the murder logically presented.

'I have to fill in some background first,' she began. 'Please be patient. To start with I must emphasize my business with Mrs Starewska was on a freelance basis. I work on several different projects including consultancy with museums. Lulu's agent, Dmitri, sourced artworks and, if he considered it worthwhile, arranged restoration for which the dealer paid in advance. Dmitri worked mainly for the Star Gallery but I later found out that he, too, had other contacts and was in the habit of trading one buyer off against another.'

'Do you have the address of this man?'

'No. I'm not even sure of his full name, but Dmitri is well known in art circles in Moscow and tracing him should not be difficult. But I very much doubt that he would cooperate in any investigation and he would, I'm sure, refuse to come to London to help with your enquiries. Shall I continue?'

'Please. I'll try not to interrupt,' Hayes said with a wry smile.

Bellamy was making notes as she spoke but Coman's pen still hovered uncertainly over his blank sheet of paper.

Tessa drew a deep breath and resumed. 'When my husband moved to St Petersburg he often brought items back to London for Dmitri.'

'Smuggling? Bellamy blurted out.

She threw a disdainful glance at Hayes' sergeant and, ignoring his question, continued, her monotone without tremor or hesitation.

'Later I learnt that one of Dmitri's clients

was a man called Kuvrov, who illegally secreted artworks in his diplomatic bag, but more of that in due course. Tony was, in effect, employed by Lulu, who had put up the money to start the car sales outlets and had, through her contacts, smoothed the path through the bureaucratic quagmire that is involved when foreign money is financing new enterprises in Russia. Capitalism is a relatively fresh concept and red tape can tie up negotiations for ever unless one knows the right people.

'Kuvrov was a "fixer" and I imagine that Lulu paid regular commissions to him to ease the Star Motors operation. I had nothing to do with all this but it was through me that Lulu first met my husband and so we became friends as well as business associates. I cleaned the icons Dmitri salvaged from the ruins of poor storage and years of neglect. Most were of average quality but occasionally an early work came to light. I have explained to you, chief inspector, the manner in which layers of paint can overlay valuable antique examples and Lulu trusted me to whittle down the old varnish and paint as I felt fit. It was a gamble and despite my experience and intuition it didn't always come off, leaving the dealer with a big bill and very little to show for it.'

She paused, eyeing her lawyer with a complicit understanding of where this was all leading. 'On that fatal Sunday I examined a painting Tony had left for me to deal with two or three weeks before. He had insisted that Kuvrov was the client, not Lulu Starewska, which struck me as odd. Why would a Russian diplomat take the trouble of sending an icon to England, when there were dozens of conservators as experienced as I in St Petersburg? Tony lied, of course, from habit, I thought at the time and—'

'Your husband knew Kuvrov?'

'Never met him, I'm sure of that, at least. Kuvrov, according to Tony, kept a low profile and dealt only through Dmitri, but my husband had his own methods and—'

'But you let it go?' Hayes gently put in.

She shrugged. 'We had our disagreements but I could hardly criticize the friends Tony made in the course of his work knowing, as I do, how important it is to keep on the right side of any civil servants. However, when I got to work on this particular icon and removed the pierced metal frame covering it, it seemed hardly worth the effort. The top painting was crude and if earlier work *did* exist it lay under several layers covering a period of perhaps five centuries and weeks of painstaking work would be involved.

However, the panel was authentic and if Kuvrov was willing to pay for an extensive restoration, so be it. But as soon as I got to grips with it, it became all too clear that the over-painting was just a cover-up. The varnish and top layer came off like a second skin revealing a masterpiece; a fifteenth-century depiction of Boris and Gleb.'

'Who?' Bellamy rasped.

'Boris and Gleb, saints of the early church canonized in the eleventh century and regarded as the true spirit of Russia. They wear distinctive clothing, fur caps and red boots that mark them out from any other saints and give them a special place. The soul of old Russia resides in such icons and Boris and Gleb are unlike the usual depictions of the Holy Family.'

'Valuable.'

'Priceless. I panicked, of course, and rushed off to tell Lulu what I had found.'

'Taking the icon to show her?'

'Good God no! I put it in the safe.'

'You didn't phone your husband about Kuvrov's icon?'

'No, of course not. Tony knew nothing about art, poor lamb. My husband was a philistine, Hayes, a lovable rogue if you like, but to him one daub was very much like another. You've seen the stuff he bought for our home when he came to live there? Terrible contemporary rubbish but Tony liked it and I really wanted to stay on at the farm so it was a done deal. We agreed to make our base at the farm if he could do a make-over, change it to a more familiar milieu for a car salesman.'

'You didn't mind?'

'I was in love. Tony is – I mean was – different from any other man I'd ever met. I accepted his son Alexei, I accepted the agreement that we had no children of our own, accepting his ghastly taste in décor was peanuts. I had the barn, a retreat I could use as I pleased and Tony was abroad most of the year, anyway.'

'You arrived at Star Cottage and found the body. What was your first reaction? Did you suspect art thieves?'

'No! Lulu never kept valuables at home. I assumed it was yet another lunatic on the loose. It was only when I phoned Tony and told him about it that I guessed he was more involved than I could ever imagine in my worst nightmares.'

Tessa's aplomb was showing cracks and her support, the ineffectual lawyer, was urging her to consider her position.

At that moment the door opened and Sergeant Preston appeared, beckoning Hayes to come outside.

'The super's had to go, sir. The interpreter's turned up and wants to get on with the Popov interview right away.'

'Has the Popov questioning started?'

'They're pushing on with it now with Mr Smyth as an observer in the viewing room. The guv'nor said you knew about it, sir.'

'Yes, that's right. Send some tea in for Mrs Cox and her brief, will you? No, make that coffee, she doesn't like our tea. I just want a quick word with Mr Smyth before he gets too involved.'

Rory was smoking a cigar, seated comfortably in the back room behind the panel that hid him from the foursome in the interview room. Waller was seated with his back to Smyth and Popov sat at the table, flexing his muscles as if for an arm-wrestling contest. The interpreter looked like any civil servant; bland, bald and a little worried.

Rory smiled. 'Like a bloody cop show this, Hayes. How's yours going?'

'Slowly. But we'll get there in the end. This woman's busy blowing her trumpet about her expertise but it looks as though she's shaping up to talk about Cox. And he's barely cold, poor devil.'

'Wifey tears of admiration?'

'Not at all. I think Tessa Cox had a shrewd

assessment of her man. Trouble is, will she try to heap all the blame on him now he's not alive to dispute it? Wait for me afterwards, Rory, I owe you dinner. I need you to make some urgent phone calls for me, if you will. See what you can dig up about this Kuvrov character, some sort of diplomatic courier. It's important.'

Thirty-one

In Hayes' absence Bellamy had taken the opportunity to grab a bite to eat, leaving Tessa Cox and her legal adviser to go over her story.

Hayes re-entered the interview room with a long list of unanswered questions on his mind but reined in his impatience, all too aware that a woman like Cox was best left with enough rope to hang herself, self-confidence being, in his experience, a hazard all too likely to snag the cocky ones. Peter Coman, the solicitor, looked more cheerful, his client having given him the boost that was supposed to come from the lawyer, not the other way around. Bellamy restarted the recording and after the usual preliminaries Hayes set the ball rolling.

'I need hardly warn you, Mrs Cox, that anything you say will be taken down as evidence.' He rattled off the required mantra before adding, 'But I'm sure Mr Coman has explained all this to you, so shall we proceed? We had got to the point where your husband, alerted by the news of Mrs Starewska's death, returns home.'

Tessa took a deep breath and picked up the thread.

'Yes, that's right. We decided to stay in London for a few days. Alexei wasn't due back until the weekend and we had things to discuss. With Mrs Starewska gone Tony's control of Star Motors in Russia was uncertain.'

'Neither of you felt any responsibility to be available for questioning?'

'No, why should we?' she snapped. 'I found the body, I was in shock. A break away from home could be regarded as a sensible move on medical grounds.'

Hayes reluctantly let this pass and nodded for her to continue.

'We heard about the fire at the gallery on the Friday and decided to come home. We returned in time to collect Alexei from his school after the skiing trip.'

'You didn't visit Mr Musset while you were in London? To discuss the problems arising from your mutual employer's murder?'

'The gallery was of no interest to Tony and I had never met Raoul Musset. The fire was a tragedy but we had enough to worry about

255

without getting involved with that.'

'Enough to worry about?' Hayes repeated. 'Your husband must have been in quite a state. He did, after all, kill himself a few days later.'

Coman cut in, legal alarm bells ringing. 'I must object, chief inspector! Suicide is the police version of this sad event. A car accident is by no means ruled out. It is for the coroner to decide.'

Hayes shrugged. 'I apologize, Mrs Cox. I have no wish to add to your distress.'

'May I continue?' she retorted. 'Yes, Tony was upset and no wonder. But it was assumed at the time that the gallery fire was accidental. We never anticipated the next disaster, Alexei's abduction. His mother is mentally unstable, the court decided she was unfit to care for her son and Vera is in no way capable of organizing a kidnap unless unscrupulous people thought we would pay a ransom and persuaded her to co-operate. The kidnap could have been planned as a result of the media coverage of Lulu's murder. The press have implied that I am seriously rich. Speculation was rife. Did Musset kill himself after finding out that his expectations from Lulu were unfounded? we wondered. Tony considered the possibility of an arson attack aimed to destroy the gallery for God knows what reason and poor Raoul Musset happened to be on the premises. All these thoughts chased round in our heads as we drove back to the farm.'

'The jury is still out on the question of Musset setting up the arson himself, Mrs Cox. So you say Mr Cox was seriously concerned about these deaths when you returned home? What did you do next?'

'Tony got a bee in his bonnet about the Boris and Gleb icon after I described the rarity of it and the fact that the over-painting had been a cover-up. After the gallery fire he decided the wretched thing was jinxed, that we should get rid of it. He said we should burn it but that would have been wanton destruction and, as a conservator, struck me as a heinous crime. He eventually agreed to hide it in the ice house, which we use for storage; a few bottles of wine and spare parts for various specialist cars Tony deals with from time to time.'

'Where is this ice house?'

'In the garden. It's a sort of underground cellar, a relic from the old days when refrigeration wasn't available. It looks like a turfed-over hillock, quite unremarkable amongst the shrubbery and the last place anyone would look.'

'You had misgivings about this superstitious idea of his, that the icon was jinxed?'

She smiled. 'Well, yes, I did. Tony wasn't the sort to get spooked by that sort of nonsense. The icon was a religious work revered for centuries and as such has a certain weird presence, I admit, but Tony was adamant that locking it up in the safe wasn't good enough. I wrapped it carefully to avoid damp and we hid it under a pile of tyres. I asked him if the owner would be coming for it but he was too distraught to give a sensible explanation then, just said it was Dmitri's problem.'

'And then the boy was taken?'

'That's right. Tony went to fetch him from his school and Mrs Edwards explained that his mother, Vera Cox, had collected him from the airport. Poor woman was aghast, of course, but at first I hoped it was just a desperate ploy on Vera's part to get more access. Then he had a phone call from the kidnappers. Tony pretended it was a business call but when we went to bed he confessed. He was at breaking point; Alexei was in the hands of the people who admitted killing Lulu and Musset.'

'He was told this on the telephone? By whom?'

'I don't know. But Tony knew who it was

and that Alexei was in terrible danger. The plan we agreed that night would have worked out if your bloody flatfoots hadn't followed him. He couldn't shake them off. Tony was pursued like a hunted animal and ended up smashed into a brick wall.'

'You are convinced it was an accident despite knowing he was the target of criminals? What had he got himself into, Mrs Cox?'

She sighed. 'Tony used to arrange transport for Dmitri, artworks to be passed on to Lulu. I found out about this only after Alexei's kidnapping as part of his explanation of the hole he was in. Possibly some of the icons Lulu passed to me for repair had come into the UK under this scam Tony and Dmitri had going.'

'Where had Dmitri got these paintings from? Were they stolen from museums?'

'Dmitri searched out these things himself, spent months touring outlying villages, persuading poor people to part with heirlooms the real value of which was unknown to them. This is a time-consuming business and any artworks found after decades of storage in damp conditions require expensive reclamation. Dmitri hit on a short cut through this government official called Kuvrov, who had access to uncatalogued items stored in museum vaults while awaiting repair and authentication. These two men, Tony explained, worked together; Dmitri had the commercial outlets, galleries in Europe and America only recently discovering the interest in icons and Kuvrov had the personal contacts. Apart from their religious sanctity icons are very decorative and much sought after by Russian ex-pats wishing to make their new homes reflect their heritage. A few fabulously wealthy Russians now collect the rare icons in the way that the eighteenth-century nobility collected Raphaels and Canalettos for their stately homes. What goes around comes around, as they say.'

'But you didn't know about this until a week ago?'

'You have my word on it. As a committed art restorer I wouldn't dream of touching anything stolen from a museum. But my poor husband was taken in by Dmitri's con and found it easy to bring in stuff that in its decayed state no one would guess was disguised under layers of varnish and paint. When the restored icons were sold to collectors in Europe, Kuvrov organized the undercover transportation and picked up substantial sums in commission, as did Dmitri and regrettably Tony, too. But this last icon, the Boris and Gleb, had been sold in advance to a Russian living in London, on photographic evidence before the over-painting camouflaged it.'

'His name?'

'Even Tony was not trusted with that but, knowing the icon was exceptional, unique, the sort of thing that would never come up for auction, Tony phoned Lulu from St Petersburg and offered to do a deal. If she could find another buyer offering a big price, Tony would swear that the icon had been "lost in transit" and even if Lulu had to compensate the original buyer for the loss the profit margin would be considerable. Unhappily, the buyer wasn't interested in compensation, he had plenty of money already, and sent his thugs to confront Lulu and recover the Boris and Gleb for his collection. Poor Lulu didn't have it and had no idea where it was. Tony hadn't told her he had already smuggled it through and had left it with me for cleaning.'

'They tortured her? Threw acid at her cat to persuade her to talk? Beat her up?'

'It would seem so. The poor darling honestly didn't know who had it but they didn't believe her and decided to search the gallery. Apparently, Raoul Musset faced the same vicious interrogation but knew nothing either and died for it. All this was spelt out to Tony on the telephone after Alexei had been abducted. You see there *was* no ransom, chief inspector. The icon was being returned to its rightful owner.'

'After a trail of blood,' Bellamy retorted.

Hayes frantically raised his hand in a calming gesture and urged Tessa to continue.

'We went over and over it that night but really there was no alternative. To get Alexei back we had to return the icon. Tony had told the kidnapper he was just the messenger boy, had no idea the icon was a masterpiece, but would return it no question. We had to pretend to the police that Tony was paying a cash ransom and on the receipt of this I would go to an appointed venue and Alexei would be handed over. We dared not risk the icon coming under scrutiny, it *had to be* handed back without the museum authorities in St Petersburg claiming it. Tony was the decoy carrying the non-existent ransom but your officers fouled up our plan and followed him.'

'He knew he was being tailed?'

'Of course he bloody did. Tony earnt a dangerous living mixing with the Russian mafia and people whose whole existence depended on security. What was he to do? The contact was told we needed time and when I got the go-ahead your lot assumed the ransom had been paid over.'

'We thought we must have missed the exchange at the motorway service station but couldn't work out how you had been told the time and place to meet up with the kidnappers before the ransom had been paid.'

'Except it hadn't. Tony piled into a wall and if any cash *had* still been in the car it went up in flames with him.'

'Did you realize you were being followed too, Mrs Cox?'

'No. I'm not as experienced as Tony at spotting surveillance. I had to agree to that girl hiding in the back of the car but chances were she wouldn't guess that the portfolio was important, it could have been anything in the dark. The tricky part had been getting it from the ice house and hiding it in the Jeep. Putting your goons on my tail was a stupid move, Hayes. If you'd left well alone I could have returned the icon as planned without a fight. By interfering you nearly cost Alexei his life and hounded my husband to his death. If you had succeeded in intercepting the icon the trail of blood your sergeant is so incensed about would have continued. Thank God one of the thugs managed to get it back to the helicopter. In the hiatus it nearly took off with Alexei. And if that poor kid had been whisked off we would never see him again. If it hadn't been for Vera pushing him out, the child would have had to live a life of a hunted animal; if they allowed him to survive, that is.'

'You make the whole set-up sound utterly ruthless.'

'After two murders, a fatal accident and a kidnapping what would you call it? These people are totally amoral, chief inspector. The man who set his heart on owning the Boris and Gleb icon would have gone to any lengths to recover his property. Nobody steals from such men and gets away with it. Accepting compensation from such as Lulu Starewska is a laughable concept. The icon had to be returned and I was determined to save it and thus save Alexei. If I have committed some misdemeanour in returning property to its rightful owner I'm sure Mr Coman here will explain the consequences to me. But, frankly, chief inspector, you don't have a leg to stand on, do you? Tony was guilty but he's dead. Lulu was implicated but she's dead. Poor old Musset genuinely knew nothing about it but he was killed anyway.'

Thirty-two

After Tessa and her lawyer had left, Hayes reported to Waller in his office. Waller looked somewhat down in the mouth and would, Hayes knew, be even more pessimistic once Hayes passed on the bad news.

'Tessa Cox is in the clear, sir. There was no ransom demand so, technically speaking, no kidnap, just a misunderstanding about the kid's pick-up. She says she was returning a stolen icon to its owner, some nameless Russian, a former oligarch, who had paid for it before it left St Petersburg and had set his men on a blood trail to collect it.'

'She knows who killed Starewska and Musset?'

'Presumably another hit man working with your prisoner. Any luck at your end?'

Waller rose from his desk and lumbered across to the filing cabinet to pour two stiff whiskies. He passed a tumbler to Hayes and slumped back in his chair.

'We shall be charging Popov with assault

to begin with. Buller's kid came up trumps on the ID parade but he's hardly the ideal witness and the prosecution isn't helped by the fact that he took so long reporting it.'

'Popov nailed to the scene shortly after the Starewska murder doesn't count?'

'We've no forensic linking Popov to the crime scene; no fingerprints, no DNA tripping him up and his knife's clean as a whistle. The right sort of knife to match Starewska's injuries but he says it's a hunting knife sold everywhere in Russia and we've checked, he's absolutely right. Two men walked into the cottage, left no cigarette butts, no saliva on the mugs or glasses, didn't even use the toilet. Clearly professionals. They put her through a vicious shake-down, stole the keys to her flat and walked back down the lane to escape in their motor boat. We've linked Kuvrov to hiring the boat and Darren Porter swears Popov is one of the men he saw down by the river that Saturday night, but that's all we've got. He can't identify the second man.'

'But Popov doesn't deny being there with Kuvrov?'

'Denies even knowing anyone called Kuvrov. Says the boat was paid for in advance by a friend of someone called Nicholai. This Nicholai was going to join them but cancelled at the last minute. Should be no problem getting hold of this mate of his, Nicholai, who proposed a bit of illicit hunting, but he'll back up Popov, no question. These guys stick together like glue. Popov says they'd heard there were wild pigs in the woods, which is true enough. That bloke at the big house rears wild boar and one or two of them stray down by the river from time to time. Nasty-looking beasts but a gourmet treat apparently. Ever tried it, Hayes?'

'Wild boar meat? No, a bit strong for me.' Hayes sipped his whisky, eyeing Waller over the rim of his glass. He had anticipated a bollocking from the superintendent, his cornering of Tessa Cox having fallen through. But his luck was in. Waller's interrogation of Popov had got no nearer to pinning down the killer, or killers, and apprehending professional hit men, especially Russian heavies, was well off Renham's normal crime sheet.

'How did Popov explain away his assault on the kid?'

'Said he thought Darren was holding a revolver, threatening his partner. He jumped him from behind but turns out it was the poor bloody kid's binoculars.'

'A gun? In Renham? I'll give this bloke

Popov top marks for thinking on his feet. What was the translator's attitude?'

'Non-committal. He's seen scum like Popov before, thinks no more highly of him than we do, but he's not going to hand over a Russian national on a plate, is he?'

'More than his job's worth, as they say. Can't you make Popov implicate this third man, Kuvrov? Where's Popov living while he's in this country?'

'Says he's here on holiday, staying in Battersea with his friend Nicholai, who will put in a character reference.'

'But he was seen staying at Vera Cox's flat.'

'Denies it. Says he saw her at the supermarket and she realized he was Russian because of the tattoos. He was just there occasionally for a bit of company and now that Vera's disappeared we can't pin him down.'

'Well, that's a load of balls for a start! He was with Vera in the helicopter. How did he explain that?'

Waller checked his notes and quoted the interpreter's words verbatim. '"My colleague, Mr Popov here, has told you that his friendship with Mrs Cox was purely sympathetic in view of her difficult situation. He suggested she collected her son for a weekend holiday at a country cottage belonging to a Russian family, friends of his living near Southampton. There was no abduction. Mrs Cox was the child's mother and was allowed time with her boy. He went with her willingly. Mr Popov knows nothing about any ransom. The helicopter flight was a treat for Alexei, a small adventure that went wrong only when the police misunderstood the arrangement. And my information is that the parents do not wish to present charges against Vera Cox." So there you have it.'

'But there was no "arrangement"!' Hayes exploded.

'No, of course there wasn't. But Popov sticks to his story that he felt sorry for the woman and the weekend away was a kindly gesture. He insists he knew of no reason why Alexei's little holiday in the country with his mother would be regarded as a police matter, and the interpreter insists that Popov stands by his version of events.'

Waller glared at Hayes, daring his DCI to question his handling of the interview. Hayes backed off.

'But he's accepted our offer of a solicitor?'

'Yes, no problem, but he's likely to plead guilty to the assault on Porter. Blames confusion in the dark.'

'It was full moon that night.'

'Was it? Still dark, though, dark enough to confuse a pair of binoculars with a weapon. He's a bloody foreigner, Hayes, can't get his head round Darren Porter's excuse that he was only a nature watcher. Don't they watch nature in Russia?'

Hayes gave up and launched into a run-down of Tony Cox's smuggling operation and the icon scam.

Waller laughed. 'Boris and Gleb? You're making it up, matey.'

'Straight up, sir. What's our next move with Cox?'

'I'll have to listen to the interview tape. We'll talk about it tomorrow. She's not going anywhere, is she? You've told her to be available for another interview?'

'She's certainly going nowhere. She's got the boy to worry about and Christmas looming. I suppose there's her husband's inquest and eventually the funeral to arrange. Are Bellamy and the lads off the hook on any possible harassment charge Cox may be threatening?'

'Skid marks on the road support our claim that Tony Cox swerved and hit the wall well ahead of our follow-up. No witness unfortunately and the suggestion that he was over the limit will be hard to prove if the body's burnt to a crisp. But a whisky bottle survived the fire so the coroner will probably take a view on it. Do *you* think he committed suicide, Hayes?'

'Well, he'd lost his job and was likely to be implicated with Kuvrov if he lived to tell the tale. It wasn't a rosy prospect, was it? According to Smyth a bullet in the head is standard practice for icon thieves. Where is he, by the way? I wanted to ask his advice about some of the stuff Tessa Cox mentioned.'

'Smyth pushed off smartish as soon as the Popov interview ended. Left a message on the desk for you saying he'd be in touch.'

Hayes was not altogether surprised to receive a phone call from Rory next morning, postponing their talk. He was ringing from the airport.

'Sorry to run out on you, chum, but I've got urgent business in Moscow, got to sort out Star Motors management before the baddies move in.'

'Can you root out anything about Kuvrov for me?' Hayes gave him a brief resume of Tessa's version of the scam Tony Cox had been involved in. 'According to Tessa, Mrs Starewska was in on it, too. Accepted goods smuggled through by Cox and sold the stuff at the gallery or through private channels. You thought she found out only recently about Cox's little game with Dmitri and Kuvrov, didn't you? You told me Tony Cox was sacked when your mother discovered what he was up to. But according to Tessa, they were all in it together.'

'I only know what she told me. Perhaps Lulu got alarmed when she heard that Dmitri's buyer was on the warpath. She liked to be in control; having Tony Cox bungling her trade methods would have gone down badly. But I'll see what I can find out, though the chances are this Kuvrov guy's well protected. Your anonymous Russian billionaire would still retain powerful contacts back home, he's not going to let a minor government official like Kuvrov squeal, is he? If Kuvrov's still alive he'll have been badly frightened by all the publicity and got himself a transfer to Siberia, or worse still, Chechnya, till it blows over. You'll never lay your hands on Kuvrov, Hayes. Think yourself lucky you've got Popov in the can.'

'But there's no forensic evidence against him.'

'Well, make it up then,' he cheerfully replied. 'Got to go, Hayes, my flight's been called.'

Thirty-three

Waller succeeded in dragging Tessa Cox back for a second grilling and insisted on interviewing her himself. But she was not to be cornered even when he confronted her with the sample of cleaning fluid Hayes had taken from her workshop and sent for examination.

'This corrosive acid is something you regularly use for your work, Mrs Cox?'

'If you stole it from my studio, yes it is. Handle it with care, superintendent, it has an awesome effect on bare flesh.'

'As Mrs Starewska's injuries proved. The men involved, and at present we are working on the theory that two men attacked her, had access to this stuff, which is, I assume, not available on the general market.'

'Indeed not. Are you insinuating I supplied these killers with acid?'

'A substance difficult to acquire, you admit. Could someone have taken samples from your barn without your knowledge?'

'I have a small boy living with me, super-intendent. I keep the barn secured at all times – there are valuable objects in my care – and any dangerous materials are kept under lock and key. I don't even allow my housekeeper into the barn, I clean it myself. There is another consideration you have not taken into account. This stuff is available to conservators like myself, and is currently used in museum labs both in the UK and elsewhere in Europe. The Americans use another brand. Whoever took this product to Star Cottage could have got it from any professional source. I don't have the mono-poly.'

Waller conceded an own goal on this one and tried to rattle his victim with questions about her husband's financial situation. 'He was well insured, Mrs Cox? Life insurance healthy, was it?'

Peter Coman stiffened and was about to interrupt but she laid a hand on his arm.

'I am well provided for, superintendent. Tony and I ran separate bank accounts and he made sensible provision for Alexei as well as myself. I hope you are not going to pursue this nonsense about a suicide, are you? I have already explained to your DCI that Tony's crazy tour was a decoy, to draw your men off my back. He was utterly exhausted by this ridiculous motorcade and had had no rest since Alexei was taken. The logical explanation is that he fell asleep at the wheel.'

'The inquest has been arranged for next Thursday, Mrs Cox.'

She drew back. 'Good. Then the coroner can pick the bones of it. Can I go now?'

Waller felt himself at a distinct disadvantage; the woman was impossible. To assuage his own dissatisfaction he continued to question her about the icon but got nowhere.

'No, superintendent, I have absolutely no idea where the Boris and Gleb icon is now nor the name of the owner. I returned it, no questions asked, sure in my own mind that until it was exchanged Alexei would remain a hostage.'

'We shall not give up on this, madam,' Waller growled.

'Is that all? May we leave now?'

Bellamy concluded the interview as Waller stormed out, Coman replacing his gold biro in his inside pocket and pulling back the chair for his client. Tessa sailed out, the two men forming a small retinue in her wake.

It was mid-February before Hayes heard from Rory Smyth again. His phone call came out of the blue and on hearing Rory's voice Hayes hesitated, wondering what had taken him so long.

'Happy New Year, Hayes!' he boomed. 'Everything hunky-dory back at the ranch?'

'If you mean have we sorted out the Starewska case, no, we haven't. Popov got off lightly and has now been whisked back to Moscow but we're still hoping to catch up with Dmitri and Kuvrov, even if it takes an extradition order.'

'Don't lose any sleep over that, old son. Dmitri's no more. Gunned down in a back street in Riga. I warned you of the likely scenario.'

Hayes' jaw dropped. 'Assassinated?'

'Well, rubbed out would better describe it. Whoever bought the icon was clearly not grateful to Dmitri for getting it back for him. Didn't want any gossip about his iffy methods of art collecting, I'd say. No good leaving a blabbermouth like Dmitri on the loose. Popov was schooled in the game, knew to keep mum, served his time without bleating. Popov is a survivor.'

'I don't suppose you could find out if a bunch of keys to your mother's flat or the cottage were found with Dmitri's effects? Or a pair of valuable icons stolen from the gallery on the night of the fire?'

Rory laughed. 'Waller said you were an optimist, Hayes. Even if Dmitri had the icons do you think he'd be mad enough to hang on to them? And supposing he did, they would disappear like snowflakes once the local police shared out the bits and pieces. It's a jungle out there, Hayes, you're on a different planet. And keys to St Bede's Square? Evidence on a plate like that? In your dreams, chum,' he said, chuckling to himself. 'But, on a happier note, how was your Christmas?'

'Terrible. I was working.'

'Me too. But I have sorted out the car sales business, greased all the right palms and left a new guy in charge. A local this time, a White Russian, so he claims. Nice manners and a discreet way with the bad boys. You ought to get yourself out here, Hayes, you'd be amazed how changed it all is. Cruise ships dock at St Petersburg all the time these days, it's not the hick town it used to be.'

'All right for rich bastards like you, Rory. My New Year break consisted of borrowing a friend's flat in Paris for a few days.'

'Not bad! You took the girlfriend?'

'Yeah, after a struggle. Christmas was the usual psychological bun fight but I was lucky, Waller kept me here on the job. You heard about Cox's inquest? Accidental death, very neat. We even managed to soft-sell the surveillance; it hardly merited a half column on the back pages.'

'Best all round, especially for Alexei. A father's suicide can leave a nasty aftertaste, can haunt a kid. By the way the good news is I managed to track down Vera Cox.'

'The boy's mother?'

'I put a private enquiry agent on it. Vera's now got a new life for herself in St Petersburg. She's linked up with her family again, has thrown off that black dog that had been poisoning her mind, all that guff about the KGB being after her. She's even got a boyfriend. I gave her a job at reception at Star Motors. Her English is good and she looks great, apart from the hair, that is. I don't know what it is with Russian hairdressers but they get terribly heavy handed with the dye bottle. Every other woman out here looks as if she's had her head in a bucket of borscht.'

'Shall I tell Tessa? She's never had a bad word for Vera, she'd be glad to know she's OK.'

'Actually, I spoke to her myself last week. I phoned to ask if she would mind if Vera wrote to Alexei now and again.'

'She agreed?'

'No problem. Being in a similar situation to Alexei when I was his age I know how losing touch with one's mother can fester if it's not handled kindly. Tessa's a sensible girl and doing a good job with the boy. It's a tricky time for a lad like him, losing his father, then his mother disappears into the sky in a helicopter, for God's sake. A little TLC goes a long way. Don't tell your superintendent about Vera being located, he might want to drag her back for questioning. He struck me as the last man to give up on a case.'

'Yeah. He's still banging on about it. Poor old Musset's the one I felt sorry for, not to say I don't appreciate your own feelings losing your mother in that way, Rory, but Musset was just an innocent bystander.'

'What's doing with the arson investigation?'

'Still being passed around the fire department.'

'What's your view on it, Hayes?'

'Luckily, it's not my case but as I see it Popov and his mate had a quick dekko at the flat, soon realized it was clean and moved on to the gallery, the last possible hiding place for the Boris and Gleb, so they thought. They put a tail on Musset and when they saw him buy a one-way ticket out to Lebanon and knew he was leaving, they blagged their way in using Dmitri's name when Musset was clearing out his personal stuff from the gallery late at night. He was a nervy type who probably guessed that your mother had been upsetting important clients in some way. He'd heard her speak of Dmitri and foolishly let them in, thinking he could talk his way clear. After all he *was* the blameless party in all this. But they started getting rough, didn't believe Musset's denials about the missing icon and Musset got badly frightened. Somehow the little guy escaped, ran upstairs and locked himself in the washroom. But he'd forgotten his mobile phone, had no way of calling for help and he could hear the pair of them ransacking the stock below. He thought, when they found nothing, they would just go away, but they set fire to the gallery, probably intended to do it all along if they brought cans of accelerant with them in the car. How about that for a likely scenario?'

Rory gave a low whistle, amused by Hayes' vivid imagination. 'Well, I'm glad you're not on the case. Evidence seems in short supply, Hayes, but it sounds plausible I agree.'

'Plausible? It's the only logical answer! And partly your fault, Rory. If you hadn't copped the lot from Mrs Starewska's estate, poor bloody Musset wouldn't have been on the spot, packing up the night the bad guys decided to search the gallery. Wicked bastards.'

'Yes, I feel bad about Raoul. Lulu should have warned him that she had changed her will, compensated him in some way. Still,' he added with a ragged laugh, 'it's water under the bridge now, Hayes. Take my word for it, there's no point in crying over spilt milk.'

'Spilt milk!' Hayes repeated in astonishment. 'Three people murdered if you include Dmitri, Cox piling himself up in one hell of a crash, and the police with no one in the dock, not a single bloody pay-off in sight.'

Thirty-four

Waller arrived at the station before nine and pulled Hayes into his office on the way through. His normally florid features were pale, his face set, and there were no bantering greetings for the early birds gathered round the coffee machine.

Hayes wondered what was up. Waller was not the brooding type, bad tempered and sunny-side up by turns, but on the whole, his moods were solidly predictable.

Hayes followed him in and closed the door, pulling up a chair and placing the latest reports on the Starewska case on the desk. The superintendent glanced through the file, his silent appraisal unnerving. Finally he shuffled the papers together and eyed Hayes with a challenging assessment.

'Nothing new here, Hayes. I'm worried. Did you see that TV programme the other night? A feature on the Starewska woman?'

'No, sir. Interesting?'

'Not my kind of show but she had plenty

of fans, including that professor young DC Robbins went to see. Stenning?'

'Yes, I think that was the name. She's back at work this week, sir, did you want a word?'

Waller shook his head. 'No. Problem is the bloody commentator made no bones about our lack of progress on the murder enquiry. Do you think we should have done one of those Crime Stopper appeals?'

'A bit late now I'd say but it's worth thinking about. We've hit a brick wall on this one, sir, and time's running out. Popov's disappeared back to Moscow and I had a call from Rory Smyth to say Dmitri, the art bloke involved in the smuggling ring with Kuvrov and Tony Cox, has been shot. Bang through the back of the head.'

Waller frowned. 'Blimey! Cox dead and now this Dmitri gunned down ... only leaves Kuvrov out there somewhere. Surely a man with a diplomatic passport can't be that difficult to find.'

'Fireproof, sir. These embassy guys are out of bounds. I've already tried to winkle out some information from the Foreign Office about Kuvrov but they won't – or can't – play ball.'

'The commissioner's concerned that the general public thinks we've let these Russians get off lightly. Political expediency.

Popov and that woman Cox was married to both scarpered.'

'Vera's been traced to St Petersburg, sir. Works for Rory Smyth at the showroom. He felt sorry for her,' he lamely added.

Waller perked up. 'You don't say! Now, there's something wicked going on and we're getting nowhere stuck in Renham. I've got permission to send one of my officers out to see if we can shake down the people in charge to let us interview Kuvrov on his home ground, at least. Could we track Popov and persuade him to lead us to Kuvrov, do you think?'

'I very much doubt that, sir. Popov's a professional, wedded to his clan. There's no bribe big enough to make it worth him throwing all that away, risking a bullet in a dark alley like Dmitri. I've asked around and judging from Rory Smyth's deep conviction of the blood tie between these guys, getting Popov to co-operate, even under protection, would be impossible. But perhaps he's still in touch with Vera Cox. Maybe she's the weak link.'

Waller fell silent and Hayes wondered if he had gone too far, pot-shotting the boss's ideas like clay pigeons.

Waller rallied. 'I propose sending you out there, Hayes, on a bit of a recce. Use Smyth only if you have to but the commissioner has organized a local back-up for us, an intelligence officer who knows the ropes. An experienced bloke called Stephenson, who would be your minder. We're dealing with dangerous people on this one, Hayes, mafia types who presumably rubbed out this Dmitri before he spoke out of turn about Kuvrov. Are you on?'

'And this is an official investigation, sir? Authorized by the top brass?'

'Absolutely. Now I am going to share a family confidence with you, Hayes, which I trust you to keep to yourself. You may have wondered how it is the commissioner and I are such good pals. The fact is...' He paused, dropping his eyes to the file. 'The fact is he's my brother-in law.'

Hayes swallowed hard, stifling a bubbling desire to laugh out loud. His fucking brother-in-law?

'A high flyer but, off duty, we keep in touch – at Christmas and so on,' he said, his voice petering out on a wistful note. Waller smoothed his tie and pushed the Starewska file back across the desk, resuming his normal gruff manner with, 'Start with Vera Cox at the garage. Pick up your air tickets from the desk tomorrow. Preston will organize some cash and this Stephenson character will fix your hotel accommodation and ferry you round the city. OK? A week should do it.'

Hayes rose and tucked the file under his arm, leaving Waller to phone for his secretary to come through.

It was only on the flight out that Hayes realized that he had forgotten to call Pippa. He sighed, wondering if this on-off romance could survive a bachelor mind set.

He was met at Arrivals by a stocky grey-haired man in a leather overcoat, who eyed Hayes' flimsy Puffa jacket with amusement while holding out a firm hand in greeting.

'Trevor Stephenson,' he said, 'but everyone calls me Jumbo – on account of my ears,' he added with a grin. 'Good flight?'

'Excellent. But it's been a bit of a race round, I was only told about this trip yesterday. You are familiar with the Starewska case?'

'Roughly. But let's push off to your hotel, we can talk later at my office. "Walls have ears", as they used to say. We're still pretty paranoid here about security, you'll soon get used to our funny ways.'

An unmarked car was parked on a diplomatic slot near the exit and the driver made like an arrow through the dense traffic. The afternoon light was gloomy and Hayes tried valiantly to attend to Jumbo's seamless commentary as they swept through the wide streets, his eyes darting from side to side, taking in the shabby apartments and the slushy crowded pavements.

'I've never been to Russia before. I didn't expect it to be so ... so...' Words failed him.

'Cosmopolitan? Times have changed, Roger. OK if I call you Roger? Your visit's too short for formalities. I've been here for twelve years. St Petersburg's like a high-class hooker; gilded and expensive where she's on show, vicious and grubby underneath. But we've suffered from such enormous changes in these last few years, things can only get better. I understand that you know the new owner of Star Motors?'

'Yes. Robert Smyth inherited Mrs Starewska's estate – the woman who was murdered. We met in the course of the police enquiries. You know him?'

'Not yet. But the social circuit here is narrow – I look forward to meeting him soon. I knew his predecessor, Tony Cox. A valued businessman here in the city – how we love our luxury limos,' he murmured with an ironic lift of an eyebrow. 'When you've settled in, Roger, give me a call on this number.' He passed Hayes his card as the car swung under the awning of the hotel entrance. 'I'll pick you up about eight thirty and we shall sample a bit of local colour before we get down to business in the morning.'

Thirty-five

The hotel was crowded with tourists, filling the foyer with their enthusiastic chatter, showing off their souvenirs. Hayes' room was modern, clean and an identikit module of hotel rooms everywhere. He showered, phoned down to room service for a steak sandwich and a bottle of vodka, and lay on the bed, trawling through the brochures and maps picked up from reception.

He called Rory's office in Moscow but he was 'out of town'. No joy there. He left a message with his secretary with the hotel number to ring back. 'I shall be in St Petersburg for a week. I'd like to see Mr Smyth before I return to England if possible.' The girl was coolly efficient, her English impeccable. Trust Rory to fit himself up with a gem.

He glanced at his watch, disorientated by the dark. Only five o'clock and Jumbo Stephenson wasn't due till eight thirty. Impatient to get out on the streets he decided to take a chance on catching Vera Cox before she went home from work. This was strictly against the rules, Waller insisting that he was not allowed to roam unescorted by his minder. But Hayes had never met Vera Cox and imagined her to be scared stiff of the police. Being confronted with two heavies would frighten a nervous woman beyond any sort of co-operation. He decided to throw the rule book away and launch out on his own.

Getting there was easy. The doorman, decked out in a theatrical Cossack outfit, whistled up a taxi and directed the driver to Star Motors. A big tip did the trick, Hayes smiling at the mental picture of Waller justifying expenses to his bloody brother-in-law, the commissioner.

Lulu Starewska's investment had clearly proved to be a landmark in the city, gleaming luxury cars spotlit in the showroom like a floor show, workers trudging home pausing to press their noses close to the brilliant display.

The cold hit him like a knife to the throat as he strolled through the forecourt to the reception area. A woman with flaming auburn hair was bent over the telephone, her thin features inexpertly made up, nervous fingers twisting a rope of false pearls at her neck. She finished the call and smiled brightly at Hayes waiting patiently at her desk. She greeted him in Russian but quickly noticed his confusion and switched to barely accented English. 'Can I help you?'

Rory had been right about the hair, the harsh dye job accentuating the dark shadows beneath her eyes, but Hayes had to admit that Vera Cox was, under the camouflage, a beautiful woman.

'The manager has left, I'm afraid. We closed half an hour ago but perhaps you would like our chief salesman to show you round before we lock up?'

Hayes discreetly produced his ID card. 'I have a message from Alexei,' he whispered.

Vera visibly paled, clutching at her pearls, white knuckled. 'Alexei? My son?'

Hayes nodded. A man in a dark suit approached, smiling broadly.

Vera launched into a flurry of Russian and the man grinned and walked off to secure the main entrance. She gathered her bag and a plastic carrier full of groceries and motioned Hayes to follow her upstairs.

Above the showroom the first floor was a maze of storage rooms plus a staff room strewn with polystyrene beakers and boxes of stationery. Vera unlocked a door at the end of a corridor and Hayes followed her into a surprisingly flashy lounge, a decorator's spree after the bare storage rooms. She relocked the door and put on the lights, depositing her shopping on a counter equipped with a two-ring hob. She turned, smiling nervously, and wordlessly indicated the sofa.

'I told Vladimir that you were my new boyfriend. Would you like some tea?'

He nodded and sat down, taking in the extraordinary décor with its midnight blue ceiling painted with stars and one wall entirely given over to smoked mirror tiles. It struck him as being a dreary bolt-hole for a girl with a history of mental illness.

Vera set a tray of tea and cakes on the coffee table and seemed more relaxed. 'You said you had seen Alexei.'

Hayes struggled out of his jacket and produced an envelope from his breast pocket. He passed it over and her face lit up with delight as the photographs tumbled out into her lap.

'How lovely!' she exclaimed, smoothing the photographs with trembling fingers. The snaps were taken in Tessa's garden a week before when Hayes arrived to pose yet more questions about the alleged kidnapping. It was a bright winter morning and Alexei, dressed in a red ski jacket, was playing with a puppy on the grass. Hayes couldn't resist snapping away at the scene, oblivious to the uselessness of such pictures to his file, but the ever-expanding case notes were so dismal that a record of the little boy who had starred in the so-called abduction could only brighten it up.

'He has a dog?' she murmured. 'Alexei said nothing to me about a dog.'

'Tessa bought it for him for Christmas. Thought it would take his mind off losing his father. You knew about Tony's accident?'

She nodded, her delight suddenly doused. 'He was not a bad man, Mr Hayes. He paid an allowance to me regularly after the divorce so I could be independent. I didn't have to work at the supermarket, it was just that my counsellor thought it would get me out of the flat, help me to get better. I had been ill, you know. I had savings, enough to return to Russia but I couldn't leave Alexei, could I?'

Hayes sipped his tea, watching the woman stroking the photographs as if her loving touch might bring the boy to life.

'Tell me about taking Alexei away. You're not in any trouble with the police, Vera, but we are trying to locate the bad men who persuaded you to pick up Alexei at the air-port. Popov still has some questions to answer. I'd like to speak to him. Are you still in touch?'

'Popov? Sergei? Oh no, I never saw him again. I thought he was in prison in England.'

'He's back home now. You were friends, I thought he might have contacted you here.'

She shook her head, the preposterous hair-do suddenly bringing back the memory of Lulu's tumbled auburn wig as she lay dead on her kitchen floor.

'But he was the one who set up the snatch, wasn't he? You met him at the supermarket?'

Her face hardened and she stared fiercely at Hayes, putting aside the photographs in a defiant gesture. 'He wasn't my lover, Mr Hayes. But I was happy to have someone to talk to. I hadn't spoken Russian to anyone except Alexei when I phoned him and when Sergei introduced himself at the check-out I realized how homesick I was. He took me to see his friend Nicholai and it was fun. I told them about the restrictions on seeing Alexei and they were very kind. Russian people are very affectionate, loving, family people, it was difficult for Sergei to understand why I was never allowed to see Alexei on my own. I was targeted, of course. I didn't realize that at the time but later it became clear to me. Nicholai and Sergei were not my friends, they used me to blackmail Tony. I don't know what was so important but, of course, this car business made Tony a very rich man, an obvious target for gangsters like Sergei.'

'He persuaded you to take your son from the school party arriving at Heathrow?'

'I knew all about Alexei's little holiday and Sergei found out when the children were expected, so it was easy. I was only borrowing Alexei for a few days, Mr Hayes, I would never have brought him back to Russia, even I know it is better for him in England.'

'But Popov organized everything?'

'He had friends with a cottage near Southampton. He used Nicholai's car and when we had Alexei he drove us to this secret place where I could be alone with my son for the first time in three years. It was too tempting to resist. I knew it was wrong but, you must believe me, Mr Hayes, I only intended to have Alexei to myself for a few days. But it all went wrong. The next night, after my boy had gone to bed, a friend of Sergei's arrived and insisted we got into this helicopter. He had a gun, there was nothing I could do. I wrapped Alexei in a duvet and we were pushed into the helicopter. The rest you know.'

Her eyes filled with tears and Hayes

ineffectually patted her hand, wondering if this unfortunate victim realized she had been the innocent pawn in Kuvrov's fight to retrieve the Boris and Gleb icon.

'Tell me how you got here.'

She blew her nose. 'I had no choice. Sergei had been arrested and the other man in the helicopter, the one with the gun, told me I must return to St Petersburg and if I held my tongue I would be safe.'

'Was his name Kuvrov?'

She gave a watery grin. 'We were never introduced, Mr Hayes. You must have seen him when everyone was fighting over Alexei. He escaped with the money in the bag.'

'He showed you the contents of the bag?'

'Oh no. The pilot and the second man just pushed me away and we soon arrived back at the cottage.'

'Could you find this cottage again?'

'I was hardly there a day or so!' she protested. 'But it was in the grounds of a big house, a dacha, I know that. We were not allowed beyond the garden, Alexei and me. Sergei stayed with us but from what I overheard I think the people at the house were very important people, very rich and dangerous, too.'

'They kept you prisoner?'

'I tried to escape but the bad man took

charge and he wasn't nice to me like Sergei. After Alexei had been rescued from the helicopter we flew back to the cottage and they arranged for me to return here. I was pushed on to a Russian merchant ship docked at Southampton. They threatened that the police would be after me for kidnapping my own son. I was terribly afraid and knew what I had done would get me into dreadful trouble, perhaps locked up in hospital again. So I decided to take my chances and return here. When the ship docked in St Petersburg I was abandoned. I had no money and no friends in the city. There was no alternative but to fall on the mercy of my sister and brother-in-law and I hitched a ride to their place near Peterhof. They have a tiny flat that they share with three children but they took me in.

'But I was lucky. Mr Smyth found me and gave me a job here. He said I could use the flat above the showroom until I found a place of my own. Accommodation is difficult here so I may have to stay in these rooms for a long time. But it is quite comfortable,' she said, waving a hand around the garish apartment. 'There is a bedroom and a shower, too. Tony used it when he was here, so Vladimir tells me.'

Looking at Tony Cox's decorative make-over, it dawned on him why it was familiar. It was a facsimile of his treatment of Tessa's family home.

Hayes rose to go, kissing Vera's hand in an impulsive gesture of sympathy. Tears brimmed afresh as she gripped his arm and led him back through the brightly lit showroom and out into the street.

Hayes ducked his head, hoping no snoopers were on his tail. By God, I'm getting as paranoid as Jumbo in this cloak and dagger game, he thought to himself.

He hailed a taxi, drawing his jacket close to his chest. When safely within the hotel he made a beeline for the souvenir shop and bought himself a furry hat with earflaps and a brightly painted Russian doll for Pippa.

Thirty-six

Hayes had just got back to his room when Stephenson phoned.

'Hi, Roger. Sorry I'm late but there's been a development. Someone has turned up who I want you to meet but he's only passing through. He contacted one of my colleagues and we've done a deal. We let him go if he co-operates with our investigation.'

'He's on the run?'

'Sort of. It's complicated. I'll tell you more about it when we meet. I have to keep this guy in custody so you'll have to make your own way to our rendezvous.' He spelt out the name of a café. 'Write it down and hand the note to the doorman. He'll call a cab for you. Roger, don't try to find the place by yourself, it's a seamen's drinking hole down by the docks. Decent food and a genuine atmosphere, not like the rip-off joints for tourists. You'll love it. The barman's a mate of mind. I'm on my way now. See you there, OK?'

Hayes changed his shirt and tried on the fur hat before the bathroom mirror, grinning at the transformation. The hotel doorman greeted him like an old friend, earmarked as a big tipper worthy of special regard.

Hayes was glad of his new headgear, the temperature had fallen below zero and a biting wind shafted across the surface of the frozen river. The taxi driver was monosyllabic, only grunting in response to Hayes' pay-off at the door of the café.

It looked a run-down sort of place to meet a high-ranking intelligence officer but a security-minded man like Stephenson obviously had his reasons and Hayes stepped inside with his fingers crossed.

An inner door was shrouded by a velvet curtain, beyond which a burly bloke smoking a pipe leant against the wall, scrutinizing the clientele who made it through the drapes. Some sort of bouncer, Hayes guessed, but the place seemed a far cry from any fancy club needing doormen.

Inside the smoke-filled atmosphere hung like a blanket obscuring what little illumination was provided. Brilliant spotlights bounced off scores of bottles ranged on shelves behind the bar and a woman accompanied by a man strumming a balalaika performed on a tiny stage hemmed in by closely packed tables, mostly unoccupied, the regular customers probably pre-warned of her dirge-like wailing. Apart from the brightly lit bar and the spotlit stage, the bistro was in almost total gloom, the wall space cut off with booths, each set up with a candle-lit table and velvet bench seats. Perfect for a lovers' assignation but, from what Hayes could discern through the dimness, the clientele was composed almost entirely of men. Perhaps the mournful chanteuse would liven things up later with a little pole dancing.

Hayes stood uncertainly at the entrance, aware that several pairs of eyes had swivelled in his direction, including the hard stare of the bartender polishing glasses. The man raised a hand and immediately Jumbo's head appeared from behind the curtain of a booth at the far end. He beckoned Hayes over.

'Sorry to leave you to your own devices first night here, old son, but we had a bit of an emergency. I've left my driver sitting in my car outside. If you park an empty motor on the street round here you'd be lucky if you came back only to find the wheels missing.'

He drew Hayes into the womb-like

interior of the curtained booth. An elderly man wearing a black overcoat with an astrakhan collar sat slumped before a glass of wine, his bloodshot eyes raised in cheerless acknowledgement of Hayes' outstretched hand. They all sat down and a waiter approached. Jumbo rattled off an order and the man returned with a bottle of vodka and a plate of evil-smelling sliced salami.

Jumbo was in great form, clearly someone with a surprise up his sleeve. 'Shall we order straight away, Roger? My friend can't spare us much time and this place gets horribly full after ten. What do you think of it? You would never have found an authentic place like this in the holiday brochures, I guarantee.

Hayes didn't doubt it. He nibbled a slice of salami to be polite but was getting a taste for the vodka and cheered up, trusting Stephenson to choose from the menu. His friend remained silent and they were well into plates of some sort of stew before the stage show was enlivened by a noisy trio. The empty seats were filling up fast and the atmosphere grew rackety with stamping feet and raucous encouragement from the floor.

Jumbo leant across to Hayes, his mood suddenly sombre. 'I trust you to keep this meeting off the record, Hayes. The situation is delicate, my involvement with my friend here something of an undercover exercise. Comprenez?'

The old man looked up, and they waited for Stephenson to continue.

'Roger, may I introduce Dmitri Lermontov?'

'Dmitri?'

Their companion laid his knife aside. 'Back from the dead,' he pronounced in barely accented English.

Stephenson jumped in. 'Shall I explain? My friend here is flying to Israel tomorrow, the news of his death being "greatly exaggerated", as they say. But before he departs he insists that his part in the Starewska scam be put to the British authorities as, in the eyes of his own government, the lies about his participation in the icon smuggling ring are sadly on record.'

'I am forced to travel on a false passport,' Dmitri put in. 'My reputation is in ruins, my life in Russia, my homeland, at an end. And all because of Kuvrov, the devil himself.' His voice quivered but the pronunciation was impeccable.

Hayes took a swig of vodka, which seared his oesophagus like a red-hot poker.

'I have very little time but I trust Mr Stephenson and I hope that *one day* my name will be cleared. You know all about Lulu's long association with Dmitri Lermontov?'

Hayes nodded, his throat paralysed by the firewater.

'Lulu and I had a perfect business arrangement for years; I found the distressed icons and she did the rest. Everything went smoothly until she got greedy. The car dealership was a gold mine and Tony Cox encouraged the silly old woman to expand the art business with the help of his wife. Kuvrov heard about me and insisted he had access to certain museum officials who could be bribed to allow neglected treasures in the vaults to "disappear". I mentioned Tony's name as I was disinclined to get involved in such dangerous exploits, but expected nothing to come of it.'

Dmitri paused, wiping a rheumy eye with his handkerchief. 'But Kuvrov made contact with Cox, although Kuvrov refused – determined to safeguard his diplomatic status – to meet him face to face and they set up a regular operation, between them smuggling many stolen items back to the gallery. I protested to Lulu but she insisted it was only by "rescuing" these damaged artworks they would be saved from total disintegration and I admitted that storage, even in the hands of experienced curators, was very, very poor. Kuvrov threatened me with a bullet if I attempted to report the thefts. A powerful man with friends in high places, or so I was led to believe.'

'But he really has diplomatic status?' Hayes protested.

'Kuvrov is now under special protection,' Stephenson intervened 'What neither Dmitri or Cox knew, and what our own intelligence unit discovered only recently, was that Kuvrov was a former Soviet agent, a "sleeper" who was given a dual identity with the ability to move around under diplomatic cover. This split personality was probably cultivated for years, from his student days in all likelihood. Dmitri and Tony Cox were duped, and we are still trying to put the pieces together and assess Kuvrov's continuing value, if any, to the present intelligence force. Cox willingly played Kuvrov's game, a little personal sideline unconnected with any spying activity as far as we know, but Dmitri here was forced to act as the middle man.

'Have you put these accusations on paper, Mr Lermontov?' Hayes interrupted.

'I have a report,' Stephenson swiftly put in, motioning Hayes to allow the old man to continue. The background noise had grown to such an extent that Dmitri found it necessary to cup his hand over his ear to catch Stephenson's mild rebuke.

'I was the expert. They needed me to authenticate their thefts, to pass them on to my dealer contacts, including Lulu. I warned her about Kuvrov and she agreed to dispense with Cox's services at Star Motors but she never met Kuvrov. If she had, my dear friend Lulu would recognize that she was supping with the devil.'

'Do you know who killed her?'

His hands trembled as he lifted his glass to his lips, his grey beard, long and untended, stained as a dribble of wine slopped down his chin. He gripped the edge of the table. 'No, I do not, sir, but it was Kuvrov who employed those thugs to torture her, to try to make her talk.'

'Talk? About what?'

'The Boris and Gleb. I had acquired this wonderful artwork from a private source we need not go into here. I showed it to Cox, who knew nothing about such things and asked Kuvrov to come to my apartment to view it. Kuvrov recognized its value immediately and, trusting in my expertise, sold it to a Russian man living in London. But Cox was a greedy man and very stupid. He took the icon from me, promising to deliver it to the Russian buyer in England but then it disappeared, probably amateurishly over-painted in order to pass it through undetected for the masterpiece it was. Kuvrov guessed that Cox had double-crossed him and through his association with Lulu sold it on. It was not Cox's property to sell. In fact Kuvrov had accepted payment in advance, and only a madman would try such a move.

'I warned Lulu but she insisted she knew nothing about any such deal, which, on reflection, may have been true. Cox's wife was a conservator. She must have been impressed by the quality of the Boris and Gleb and the two of them decided to sidestep Kuvrov and sell it on to a higher bidder. I was not involved in this disgraceful deceit but I was caught in the middle, the only one who could pinpoint Kuvrov and expose the dishonest museum curators who were bribed to release icons from the storage vaults.'

The old man was sweating profusely and Stephenson poured him a glass of water from the carafe, glancing at Hayes with a frown of concern. But Dmitri was in full flow, anxious to put his side of the story.

'Cox's theft of the icon set in motion Kuvrov's mission to retrieve it, starting with

Lulu Starewska, who he knew to be Cox's outlet at her London gallery. She was killed by Kuvrov's men, who continued the search by moving on to the gallery. When I heard about Musset's death I knew I had to disappear, escape from Kuvrov's gangsters. But I am an old man, and they traced me to Tallinn. From there I fled to Riga and spent my savings bribing a police inspector I know there to stage my death, using a tramp's body as my double. My life as Dmitri Lermontov is over. I am Felix now and, with God's grace, I shall end my days with my brother and his family in Jerusalem.'

Hayes caught Stephenson's eye and shrugged. Such an implausible story. But was it? Was it really possible to stage one's disappearance like that? In Riga perhaps it was. He waited for Stephenson to wade in but, at that moment, the velvet curtains at the entry blew inwards and a tall figure in a camelhair overcoat picked his way through the now-crowded tables and thumped Hayes on the shoulder.

'Hayes, old man. What on earth are you doing in this dump?'

It was Rory, even larger than life in this back-street Valhalla.

'I got your message from the office and I drove straight to your hotel, a favourite watering hole of mine. Took a matter of minutes to shake down that bloody doorman. Remember, Hayes, it's always good policy to keep in with hotel doormen. Yours is a long-term mate of mine. Ivan the Terrible, I call him, told me straight off where I could find you, showed me your handwritten note or I wouldn't have believed the bastard. So here I am. Small world. I happened to be in town for a meeting, couldn't pass up the chance of a night out with my chum Hayes, could I? Won't you introduce me to your friends?'

Dmitri rose, pushing Stephenson aside, drawing his hand from his overcoat pocket as if, Hayes thought, to shake hands. A shot rang out, then another, and Rory went down like a felled ox, a chair smashing into splinters as he cannoned into it. Instantly all the lights went out and the whole place was thrown into darkness, only the candles on the tables showing puny halos of flame.

Hayes felt a hand gripping his arm, shoving the old man ahead of him towards the exit.

'Quick! Get him out of here, Roger. My car's right outside. Tell the driver to shoot you back to the hotel. Drop Dmitri off on the way. I'll stay here and clear up this mess.'

Thirty-seven

The place was in uproar, screams punctuating the stampede to the exit. In the midst of the rabble trying to escape, Hayes kept a tight hold on the old man and shoved him through the car door held open by Stephenson's driver.

'Drive on!' Hayes shouted. 'The boss will follow, OK?'

They set off with a squeal of tyres, Hayes steadying Dmitri as they were flung about as they raced away from the docks, back towards the city.

Dmitri leant forward and shook the driver's shoulder. 'Drop me at the Church of the Spilt Blood,' he croaked. 'I'm safer on foot.'

'Not on your life, mate. You've just shot a friend of mine. What's the game?'

Dmitri stared at Hayes in disbelief. 'You're one of them? You're with Kuvrov?'

'Kuvrov?'

'That devil. That man was Kuvrov. Stephenson set me up, didn't he? Knew I was going to kill Kuvrov before I departed from the airport. Why else would I risk appearing in this city – as a ghost?'

Hayes felt nauseous, the vodka shots jolting his thought processes like jumping jacks.

'Stephenson didn't even *know* Rory – he was *my* friend. You're tragically mistaken, Dmitri. You've just killed the wrong man.'

Dmitri drew the gun from his pocket and laid it on the seat beside him. 'I have never shed blood before tonight but I had sworn to eliminate that man before I departed this life. Stephenson wasn't interested in justice, he just wanted to use me as a lever against Kuvrov, allow him to live in exchange for certain co-operation. I know these people, truth died in this city long ago. It *was* Kuvrov, my friend, you are the one who was deceived. But I must go,' he said, half rising in his seat as the car drew into the kerb. The pavements were still crowded and before Hayes could stop him Dmitri had jumped out, surprisingly spryly for an old man, and disappeared into the shadow of an enormous church. The driver accelerated away, Hayes' urgent remonstrations ignored. Wasn't Dmitri supposed to be in custody? His brain slopped about in his skull like dishwater and when the car drew up at the hotel the vital necessity was to get to his room and throw up the salami and stew that Jumbo's ghastly night out had presented.

He lay on the bed fully clothed, the room undulating like a merry-go-round, the night's events churning in an endless charade behind his closed lids.

The knock on the door woke him with a start. The police? What was he to say? Why had he bolted from the scene of a crime? And what about losing Dmitri, a man already in custody, for God's sake; Stephenson's bloody star witness turned assassin?

The knock came again more urgently. Hayes rose, his head pounding. 'Yes? Who is it?'

'Open the fucking door, Hayes. It's me. Jumbo.'

He stumbled to the door and Stephenson burst in. 'Where's Dmitri?' he barked.

'You said to drop him off. I couldn't stop him, leapt out like a bloody gazelle at a church in the centre. Spilt blood? That can't be right.'

'He was supposed to stay overnight at a safe house – but we can probably pick him up at the airport in the morning.' Stephenson sat down, panting like a man just a bit too old for all this. 'The Church of the Spilt

Blood you say? That figures.' He smiled, relaxing at last. 'An appropriate exit, eh?'

'You're not worried? He was in your charge. Did you know he planned to kill Kuvrov?'

'Well, as a matter of fact I did. Plan was to head him off, push him straight on the plane. We already had all the information we needed, Kuvrov was no mystery to us, just a few missing pieces that Dmitri kindly stacked up for us.'

'You are saying Kuvrov's alter ego really was Rory Smyth?'

'We suspected him months ago but were pretty sure his days as a useful Russian agent were long gone. But when he popped up as the new owner of Star Motors my boss had a brainwave. Moving with the high rollers as the proprietor of a business like that, Mister Robert Smyth was soon persuaded to help us out with one or two things.'

'Turn double agent?'

'Well, yes. We got a tip-off about Dmitri's false identity and arrested him to use as a lever to incriminate Smyth in the Starewska murder.'

'But I knew Rory. He wouldn't have ordered his mother's death, he owed everything to her.'

Jumbo shrugged and crossed the room to pour himself a stiff vodka from Hayes' depleted bottle. 'How long have you known this guy? Weeks? Months? As Kuvrov he had a long association with the low-life here. Sending thugs to prise the whereabouts of the icon out of the old lady was possibly par for the course. He might even have deluded himself that their aim was achievable without beating Starewska to death. You have to remember that Kuvrov was seriously afraid of this anonymous Russian buyer who had paid for the sodding icon and was not the sort to accept that there had been a cock-up and his purchase had been gazumped, as it were. Kuvrov had to get it back at any costs and, having perfected this split personality over the years, may well have seen a benefit from the disappearance of the old girl. You and I assume a man would never kill his own mother but what do we know? And as a cynical old pro I can't ignore the fact that Smyth stood to inherit two valuable car dealerships and Christ knows what else if the poor cow died. Retrieving the icon was vital but, with the old lady gone, he could enjoy the high life in Russia, which I suspect was the location that most appealed to him; a big noise fitting in with the nouveaux riche in Moscow as he could never be in London.'

'I'm still sceptical, Jumbo – he seemed such a nice bloke.'

'Well, on the cultural level old Mrs Starewska was stripping heritage items from Old Mother Russia after all. And from what I found out about Smyth he was abandoned as a kid by the very woman who later used him as a go-between for her profitable business ventures. Rough justice?'

Hayes tried to absorb all this, wondering how he could frame any sort of report for Waller. 'What about Dmitri? How did you resolve the business of the shooting tonight?'

'All perfectly simple,' Jumbo said with a smile of satisfaction. 'The scenario goes like this, so listen up. You and I met for a lively evening out and by chance this friend of yours, Robert Smyth, alerted by the hotel doorman, tracked us to the bistro. The place is a notorious hellhole and in the darkened room Smyth was mistaken for a mafia boss called Beloff, who swanks round town in a camelhair coat. I told the local fuzz I'd sent you back in my car for safety and they are quite happy with my explanation. You may be called upon to verify it but so long as we sing from the same hymn sheet we're home and dry. No one saw Dmitri with us, OK?'

'How's that?'

'The owner wants no aggro with the police and the barman's seen it all before. As soon as there's any sort of fracas he switches off all the lights and those with something to hide get out quick. The ambulance took your friend away.'

'Rory's alive?'

'Not a hope.'

Hayes' mind was beginning to clear at last. 'Tell me, why didn't Rory recognize Dmitri as soon as he walked in?'

'The beard's new. Old Dmitri Lermontov was a smart, international art dealer before Kuvrov got his claws into him. The old boy was destroyed when his reputation went down the pan; gossip is rife in that line of business, and he certainly looks a broken man. Smyth would have caught on pretty quick but Dmitri was on a hair trigger, took his chance and "Bam!!"'

'Did you know he had a gun?'

'Hell, no. But it doesn't surprise me. Dmitri faked his death and was taking a chance coming back to Russia at all. He should have scarpered straight from Riga but there was unfinished business. Revenge is sweet if your life's work is trashed by a bully like Kuvrov.'

'I feel I put Rory's head on the block myself...' Hayes muttered. 'I liked the guy, Jumbo. Had my doubts from time to time but he was so plausible – or perhaps I haven't learnt to be suspicious.'

'My job's made me a miserable sod in some ways. You get into the habit of watching your back. I'll square it with the authorities here before you fly out, but a brief statement's all they'll need. I suggest you go back to England as soon as possible. Your investigation's over, chum.'

'But the Starewska murder. How do we draw a line under that? We've no evidence against Popov, we don't know the identity of the second man and Kuvrov's dead. How do I explain Rory's double life to my boss?'

'Don't. It's top secret, our intelligence information will not be linked. Just stick to the facts, no embroidery; Smyth followed you to the bistro and got shot in a situation of mistaken identity. The Russian police are seeking the man who pulled the trigger but Dmitri Lermontov *does not exist*. Got it?'

'There were no witnesses? No one saw Dmitri point the gun? The waiter doesn't remember serving him?'

'No one saw a thing,' Jumbo insisted. He rose to go, leaving Hayes with the burden of secret information that would never allow him to claim to have solved the Starewska murder. Life was a bitch.

In the plane home Hayes toyed with the wooden Russian doll he had bought for Pippa, revealing the tiny hidden figures stacked one inside the other. It was a very Russian concept, a gaily painted subterfuge, not really a toy at all.